TAINTED SAINT

A HAWKE FAMILY STORY

BILLIONAIRES OF NEW ORLEANS: THE HAWKE
FAMILY
BOOK 5

GWYN MCNAMEE

TAINTED SAINT by
Gwyn McNamee © 2018

Cover Design: Michelle Johnson at Blue Sky Designs

❀ Created with Vellum

To anyone struggling with guilt or insecurity...remember, everyone deserves a happily ever after.

ACKNOWLEDGMENTS

Thank you to everyone who helped with Saint and Caroline's story who may not get a specific mention.

To my BFF and favorite Jamaican Aileen, thank you for all the amazing into on your home country and for helping me make Saint more authentic.

To my betas, thank you once again for providing invaluable feedback about the story.

And to my husband and daughter, thank you for giving me the support I need to keep writing.

PROLOGUE

CAROLINE

Only one word comes to mind when I picture Saint Clarke.

Adonis.

There's no other way to describe him nor could anyone else ever compare to the man. It's hard to compete with six-five, three-hundred pounds of pure muscle and raw sex appeal. Even when he's trying to remain as inconspicuous as possible standing by the door at the club, his presence fills the room.

The man is just...hot.

Really fucking hot.

Since the moment I first stepped foot into TWO and saw him working the door, I haven't been able to keep my mouth or lady bits from watering every time he's in the vicinity. I'm like a bitch in heat, and I'm not ashamed to admit to myself...I would climb that man like a damn tree.

And he's here at the party tonight...

I'm on the hunt. Like I told Storm not an hour before she disappeared, it's open season.

Why come to a party like this if you're not going to enjoy yourself?

Which is why I was counting down the seconds as Jennifer prattled on and on about *An Intimate Affair* and the parties, and the setup, and membership, and all the other tedious details I'll probably need to know to write my story. The recording on my phone ensures I didn't miss a single thing even though my mind was somewhere else entirely.

With him.

And now that I have what I came for, it's time to get what I want.

This masquerade ball gives me the perfect excuse to approach Saint as someone else...anyone else. I can't do it as Caroline—best friend of his boss' wife. That's just...awkwardness in the making.

But then again, he probably doesn't even know who I am, anyway. I don't think we've ever spoken more than two words to each other when I've been to the club, and Dani and I spend more time at the main club than at TWO anyway. That's probably a good thing, though, because if I did try to talk to him, I'd be a blubbering mass of nerves.

I'm not Dani. I can't just walk up to a guy under normal circumstances and tell him I want to fuck. But here, tonight, in this place, anything's possible. I can be anyone I want. I can do anything I want. And what I want to do is Saint.

If I can find him...

Where did he go?

It's hard to hide a man that size, yet five minutes of searching have resulted in nothing but frustration on my part.

I push up on my tiptoes in my heels and scan the crowded room full of sex and debauchery. This party really is something else. It's the best assignment I've ever received from the paper for sure. And the night will only get better. If I can find the object of my affection.

He should tower above everyone. He should be impossible to

miss. Yet...nothing.

I slump back down and adjust the mask covering the top half of my face.

Shit. I hope he didn't leave while I was talking to Jennifer.

That would be a major let-down after what has been a very eye-opening evening. One that's left my body vibrating with need. Watching all these people have sex, it's impossible not to be affected.

Come on...live porn!

Warm breath flutters against my neck. "Looking for someone?" The deep voice rumbles next to my ear and a hard, huge body presses against my back.

I swallow against my suddenly dry throat and turn my head to look over my shoulder.

The search is over. It seems the man himself found me.

A shiver of anticipation rolls through my primed body.

Be decisive. Be aggressive. Take what you want.

This may be the only chance I get, so I need to take advantage while I can. I suck in a deep breath and turn to face him. Mere inches separate his massive barrel chest from my face.

Christ. He's huge.

And he asked me a question. If I was looking for someone...

I tilt my head back to look up at him.

Deep breath, Care.

"Yeah. You."

He flashes me a dazzling white smile beneath the red masquerade mask covering his eyes and leans down until his lips brush the shell of my ear. "What a coincidence. I've been looking for you too, since the moment you walked through the front door."

Christ...

Moisture floods between my legs as the promise in his words reverberates through my chest.

"Why is that?" My question comes out raspy...sexy...and so

unlike me. I meet his warm brown eyes. His lips tilt up in a lopsided grin, and his hands curl gently around my biceps.

"The only reason someone would be here." He nods back down the hallway behind us. "Come."

His giant hand slides down my arm and engulfs my tiny one, and he leads me toward the private rooms Jennifer showed me earlier.

Oh, my God. This is actually happening.

My stomach flutters with more nerves than I had on prom night as he holds the door open and ushers me in with a large hand at my lower back. The cool air in the room sends goosebumps spreading across my flesh, but the heat of his touch keeps me grounded in the here and now.

The Caroline who never initiates, the one who talks a big game but usually stands back and lets someone come to her isn't here. This mask creates a new Caroline. This Caroline isn't afraid to take what she wants.

A massive platform bed dominates the center of the room, with a chaise to the left and an array of sex toys laid out on the table to the right. I gulp as the overhead lights reflect off the metal and make the leather shine.

Oh my...

The door clicks shut behind us, and Saint tugs me across the room. His eyes follow mine to the toy display, and he laughs. "Don't look so scared. While I would really love to play with you some time, I have something else in mind for tonight."

I suck in a deep breath and press my thighs together against the throb his words elicit. He walks me backward until my knees hit the bed.

"Ooh!" A little gasp slips from my lips followed by a nervous giggle.

He leans down and brushes my hair back from my cheek before he presses his lips to the sensitive spot behind my ear. "You ready for this?"

Holy hell.

I thought I was.

SAINT

I'm so ready for this. Having Caroline here, quivering in my arms, is everything I've dreamt about since the first time I saw her. Her honeysuckle scent invades my every breath, and the sequins of her black floor-length gown scratch against my palms as I hold her against me.

The tiny woman who has occupied my fantasies for so long stares up at me from behind her black mask, the crystal green eyes filled with lust and maybe a little trepidation. I grasp her chin and brush my thumb across her lips.

"I won't hurt you. I promise nothing but pleasure for you tonight."

Pleasure for her and me.

My cock strains against the front of my pants as I press it into her stomach. She moans, and I lean down to taste her lips for the first time.

Sweet. Divine. Everything Caroline.

When my eyes found her tonight, my cock raised to attention for the first time since arriving at the party. It's been a long time since a woman could affect me.

On a night like this, in this environment, it's the perfect time to let go of any inhibitions, any reservations. No way I would miss this opportunity if she's willing.

And she is certainly that. The moment her eyes met mine and she told me she'd been looking for me, it was a done-deal.

Caroline Brooks is finally mine.

Even if only for one night.

I press my lips to hers as my hands work her dress up around her slim but shapely hips, exposing her bare pussy to me.

No panties.

Fucking perfection.

My palms glide over her smooth, pale skin, leaving goose-bumps in their wake.

I press a kiss to her neck and revel in the shudder that rolls through her as her arms wrap more tightly around my neck. "How do you want me?"

She whimpers, and the warm flutter of breath spreads across my heated skin. My cock throbs.

"Hard?"

"Yes."

"Fast?"

"Yes."

"Now?"

"God, yes."

Her hands move to my waist and drag down the zipper on my pants. My cock springs free, and her small, warm palm wraps around the base.

Fuck.

I grab a condom from the bowl sitting on the table next to the bed and hand it to her while my lips find hers again.

Demanding and needy, the kiss mimics every damn thing I want to do to her tonight.

She releases my cock for a second, then slowly slides the condom down my length. The brush of her fingers is enough to almost have me coming on the spot.

Christ.

I've waited so long for this. For her.

And she has no idea.

She's always been so aloof, so out of my league. So untouchable.

But tonight...everyone's on a level playing field.

I'm not just a washed-up football player turned bouncer, and she's not a respected journalist. We're just two people bound together by desire and need.

I pull away from her mouth and take her chin in my hand, tilting her face up to mine. Her pale green eyes flash at me.

My hand snakes down between us, but I pause at her waist. "Turn around, if you're ready for me."

"I'm more than ready." Soft, breathy words.

Exactly the ones I've been dying to hear from her sweet mouth.

She turns and climbs onto the bed, her elegant gown bunched up around her hips and that mask still in place over her face.

I'd give anything to see all of her—no dress, no mask, nothing hiding ourselves—but not tonight. She's not ready for that, otherwise, we would have been doing this a long time ago.

I brush the head of my cock through her slick core, and she shivers and shifts back, offering herself up to me under the bright overhead light.

"Fuck, you're beautiful."

She whimpers softly and reaches back to guide my cock inside her. Wet heat wraps around me, and she clenches down.

Fucking heaven.

Through gritted teeth, I drive into her and dig my fingers into her exposed hips to keep her in place.

Her head drops down to the bed. "Oh, God!"

Watching my cock disappear inside her has my balls and spine tingling. I want this to last forever, but it's going to come to an explosive end soon for both of us. Far too soon.

If only this party could go on and on and I could stay inside Caroline until my dying day. I would die a happy man.

Her hot, wet pussy wrapped around me, sucking me inside her and holding me captive...it's the only place I want to be.

She clenches around me again. "Faster."

Hell...

I lean forward and nip at her ear. "Whatever you need."

I'll give her anything she asks for, anything she wants, anything she ever needs.

If I could only tell her that, but I don't dare utter a word of it tonight. Not in a place like this. Caroline needs the anonymity to let go, and I won't ruin it for either of us.

Her hips slam back to meet my thrusts, driving me even deeper as I increase my pace. Slapping flesh and our panting breaths fill the room—a song for only us.

One that will replay in my head every day after this.

There's nothing but the feeling of her body and mine. Soft skin. Wet heat. And the sounds of both of us getting and giving each other everything.

She stills, then cries out. "Oh, fuck."

Her pussy ripples and clutches at my cock as I drive into her again and again, chasing my own ecstasy.

It washes over me with a blinding light and heat that rolls through my limbs. My fingers dig into her soft flesh, and I grit my teeth as I come.

When I finally still, she collapses on the bed, and I brace myself over her. Tiny puffs of breath slip from her parted lips, but her eyes stay closed behind that mask.

Spread out like this, with that mask, in this dress, she looks more like a Renaissance painting than anything real, but she is real. Very real. And I want her more than I've ever wanted anything in my life.

This hasn't sated my desire for her. The burning need I've felt for so damn long still lingers in my chest.

This woman...

I lean over her and press my lips to her warm cheek. She moans softly and shifts but doesn't open her eyes. "That was magnificent. Let's do it again."

Her eyes flutter open, and a smile breaks out across her face. "Whatever you need."

1

ONE MONTH LATER

SAINT

Afull week of babysitting and watching Storm. A week of being on guard and having my life revolve around protecting one person. And it was all for nothing.

That crazy woman still managed to sneak up on us and ruin Storm's life. And it had nothing to do with Dom and everything to do with Landon's past.

We were all focused on the wrong damn threat.

I growl and slam my fist into the steering wheel. I haven't had a drop of alcohol in over five years, but this entire situation has me on the edge of driving to the club, not to work but to access the amazing selection of booze behind the bar. Drowning my sorrows was always my go-to way to cope, and there's only one other way to do it without alcohol—Caroline.

She's everything I ever wanted, and that party was a fucking dream come true. What we shared that night was incredible...but when it was over, she turned her back and disappeared into the night.

She has no idea when I saw her there, my heart stopped and my breath caught in my chest; that it's been that way since the first time she ever set foot into TWO. No idea that she's so far out of my league that the mere thought of approaching her before was out of the question.

No idea that I knew *exactly* who she was.

And there's no doubt she knew it was me. It's hard to hide behind this body. Yet, she never said a word. Never acknowledged who I was or who she was.

She gave in to me and gave herself to me completely in that short time. Then got up and walked away without a backward glance.

Did I totally misread her? Was it really just a one-night stand?

Probably. What would she want with a guy who throws drunks out on their asses when they harass the naked girls or get too far out of line?

Caroline is beautiful, elegant, well-educated, and has an important job at a reputable newspaper. I can never have her. Not really. Not permanently. Yet when I take my cock in hand to stroke myself, it's her I envision. Her I see bent over my bed with her ass high in the air. Her riding me.

Shit.

I shake my head and pull over to the side of the road.

Where the hell am I even going?

When I heard about what happened at Storm's tonight, I climbed in my car mindlessly with no destination planned. I drove...and now, I can't even remember what streets I've been on since I left the condo.

Christ. I hope I didn't do anything stupid like run a red light while I was spaced out.

I scan the area to try to get my bearings. I'm only a few blocks from the club. Going there and working, even though it's my night off, might help clear my mind of how I failed Storm, failed the Hawkes, failed the only family I have here in the States. It may help me rid myself of visions of Caroline sprawled out on the bed in rapture. It could help vanquish her cries of pleasure echoing in my ears and the way she begged for more.

Maybe, just maybe, work will help me forget.

The parking lot looks strangely empty without Savage and Gabe's cars. They're undoubtedly with Storm right now, dealing with the fact that her damn house just burned the fuck down...

Because of me.

I slam the car into park and climb out into a light drizzle.

The door into the club swings open easily, and Tubbs' eyes widen when they connect with mine. "What are you doing here? You aren't on the schedule."

"I know, but I figured you could use an extra hand. Are Savage and Gabe gone?"

He nods.

By now, the whole Hawkeye Club crew has to know what happened with Storm. They have to know my failure. Their knowing eyes judge me for what I couldn't do—keep her safe.

I move to step around Tubbs, and one of his large hands falls on my shoulder, stopping me in place.

His darks eyes soften with empathy. "It wasn't your fault, man."

Bullshit, it wasn't.

"You don't know what you're talking about." I shrug off his hand and make my way to the bar were Byron stands, looking a little fazed staring at the bar top. I grab a stool in front of him, but he doesn't even look up. "Byron?"

Confused eyes meet mine, and he blinks and shakes his head. "Shit. Sorry, I didn't see you there. Did you hear about Storm?"

I nod, and all the color drains from his face. He looks like he's about to puke. "What's wrong with you? You don't look so good."

He lets out a low, humorless laugh. "I fucked up, dude. I really, really fucked up."

"Not as badly as I have. This all happened to her because of me." Earlier today, I followed Luca Abello into this very building for a meeting and then I let Landon and Storm leave without any protection. I was so fucking stupid.

"That's not what I'm talking about. That wasn't your fault. Landon never told anybody about his wife. He never told anybody his history. No one could've anticipated it, let alone prevented what happened. We all thought it was Luca." He slams the bar. "We had every reason to believe it was Luca. No one can let their guard down around that man. Not ever."

It almost sounds like he's speaking from personal experience but...

That's impossible.

"I agree. I don't trust the guy. I'll be keeping a close eye on the club. Even before this shit happened with Storm tonight, Savage and Gabe asked me to move over here to the main club as some added protection since they're here most often."

He sighs and nods as he looks down the bar toward a couple at the end. Their drinks still look full, so he returns his attention to me. "It's probably a good idea. That why you're here now?"

I run my hand back over my head. "No. I was just out driving, thinking, and ended up here." Hoping doing something mindless like checking IDs and watching out for pervs would help me push away the guilt and everything else jumbled up in my head.

He snorts and waves a hand back at the rows and rows of bottles behind him. "I would offer you a drink but..."

Yeah. Maybe coming to a bar wasn't the greatest plan.

The guys know I don't drink. And they know why.

A grin tugs at my lips. "A Coke with a slice of lime would be great."

He smacks the bar. "Coming right up. So, is it the Storm business that's got you out of sorts tonight?"

"The Storm business..."

Almost getting her killed by letting my guard down and assuming things were okay. When I first started working in private investigation and protection after the league, one of the first things I learned was never to assume anything. Yet, I made that mistake, and she paid for it. "Among other things."

My drink appears in front of me, and I squeeze a lime into it.

Some Jack in this would be nice.

"Would those other things be a woman?"

I chuckle and stir the drink with the tiny straw in it. "That obvious?"

"I've worked here for a long time. When men come in looking like you do, it is most often because of a woman. Almost without fail. What did this one do to you?"

I shrug and take a sip as I try to figure out a way to explain it. "Nothing, actually. Nothing bad, anyway. She did exactly what we were supposed to. I guess I had just hoped for...I don't know..." I shake my head, "more?"

He barks out a laugh and shakes his head. "I thought men were supposed to be commitment-phobes?"

"That's never been true for me. When I was still playing, I was involved with a woman and very much committed."

"What happened?"

I asked myself that question a hundred times after Jenna left, but only one answer ever rung true. "I got hurt, and she saw the money going out the window and didn't want to be stuck on a sinking ship."

Byron recoils, and a long, slow whistle slips from his lips. "Damn, bro, that's harsh."

"It is, but she was right, wasn't she? I mean, God, I love it here. I love the Hawkes and everyone else, but I'm a damn bouncer. It isn't exactly the lavish lifestyle she was accustomed to when I was playing."

His eyes narrow on me, and a single eyebrow rises. "Does it have to be? For her to be happy?"

"Her? Yes."

"What about the current woman? Is that the issue?"

"There are a lot of issues. And that may very well be one of them, but I guess I'll never know."

"You're not gonna pursue her and try to figure out a way to make things work?"

It's crossed my mind a million times since the party to do just that. Walk right up to her at the club or go to her office and come right out and tell her I want her.

Out in the open. Not just behind masks and illusions of being different people.

I just don't have the balls for that right now. Not after what happened with Storm.

It feels like I've been castrated and had them shoved down my throat to choke me.

CAROLINE

"Hello, Earth to Care?" Dani raps her knuckles against the granite counter.

"Huh?"

She narrows her eyes from across the kitchen island and scowls. "Where were you just now? Because it sure as hell wasn't here. You haven't heard a word I said."

Nope. Not a single word.

It was kind of like the teacher from Peanuts *waah, waah, waahing* in the background as I stared into my wine for the last five minutes. I could lie and pretend I did hear her, but it would be pointless. Dani knows me too well for me to get away with that.

So instead of mustering up that lie, I take a large glug of wine. The crisp liquid slides down my throat but doesn't offer me a good explanation for why I've been so spacey.

"Sorry, I'm just a little distracted."

Her eyes soften. "Are you worried about Storm?"

"Aren't you?"

While Savage, Gabe, and Skye raced over to help Storm and Landon with anything they might need tonight, Dani and I are left here waiting while Kennedy sleeps down the hall.

She sighs and pours herself another glass of wine. "Of course, I am, but Savage assured me she's fine. He said she's handling things remarkably well considering."

"Good. I'll call her tomorrow, when things have calmed down a bit. See if she needs anything."

"I'm sure she'll appreciate that."

It will give me something else to focus on too. Because lately, all I've had on my mind whenever I'm not working is *one* thing. Or rather...*one* person.

A big man with a beautiful cock who knows how to use it.

It's been weeks since my one night with Saint. The one night I was able to free myself from any inhibitions. One night I was able to be someone else. It was supposed to fulfill that damn need and get it out of my system.

Yet, I can't stop thinking about it.

The way he touched me. The way he whispered dirty things in my ear while he pounded into me. The way he drove me to oblivion over and over again for the few short hours we had together.

That man can fuck. There's no doubt about that. But it was so much more...

Hard and soft. Fast and slow. Brutal and gentle. It was so much more than I even imagined was possible.

There was something else there.

A pull. A spark. A connection. One that scared the shit out of me so badly, I flew out of there as fast as my short legs and high heels could carry me once we were done.

The mask may have hidden my identity, but the way Saint was looking into my eyes, it was almost like he could see into my soul.

And that won't do. That can't happen.

I can't be with Saint Clarke.

Dani sips her wine and twirls the glass in her fingers. "Anyway, I was asking if you wanted to come to the club with me on Friday night. Savage and I are finally going to have a date night. My mom is watching Kennedy, and I'm thinking we could go early and have a couple drinks before he and I leave."

A night out and some drink sounds amazing. Dani and I barely see each other anymore now that she has Kennedy, and I've been busting my ass the last several weeks on various stories.

Ever since the party, I really haven't had a chance to unwind. And certainly not in *that* way. Drinks will be a sad substitute, but it's better than being home alone and wallowing in the boringness that is my life.

"That sounds good."

Better than good.

She waggles her eyebrows at me. "Savage says we should take the car service, so I'll pick you up around six. I think our dinner reservation is at eight so that gives us a little bit of time."

Just a few measly hours before I go back home alone to watch shows in my sweatpants.

I should be excited, but I can barely muster up a fake smile. "Great."

She narrows her blue eyes on me. "Seriously, Care, what's wrong with you? You've just seemed off the last couple weeks."

Having a best friend is great, until they can read you like a book and you don't really feel like revealing you're disenchanted with life, your job, and had a one-night stand with her husband's employee.

The old Dani would have been down to gossip about that, but I'm not so sure married mom Dani will be as excited to hear about my escapade.

I've managed to convince her I went to the party, met with Jennifer to get what I needed for the story, and that was the extent of my evening. Since she's so damn good at knowing I'm lying, either she's letting me get away with it, or she's slipping.

I sigh and swirl the wine in my glass. "I guess I have been."

It's been an endless loop of work, eat, Webflix, sleep. Repeat. The days all blur together into a kind of timeless mush.

Is this really what being an adult is all about? If so, it sucks.

"What's going on?"

"I'm not entirely sure. I guess it's the big birthday coming up..."

Dani barks out a laugh and rolls her eyes. "You're only going to be thirty. It's not the end of the world."

I glower at her. "That's easy for you to say. You're not thirty for another couple years."

She flashes me a grin and winks. "Nope, old lady, I'm not."

Bitch.

"Ha. Ha." If it were anyone else, I'd be pissed, but this is just Dani. And she's worried about me. "I don't know, it just seems like everybody is settling down, and, you know, finding their futures while I'm still working the same job I've been at since I graduated college and going to bars and clubs to meet dudes. Alone, I might add, since you found your happily ever after."

Dani takes a sip of her wine and leans forward to rest her elbows on the counter. "There are lots of ways to meet people, Care. I mean, online dating is how one in five marriages start these days."

Blech.

I stick my tongue out. "You know me. I can't do the whole online dating thing. I have to meet somebody, see them in person to know if there's a spark there. I'm not going to waste my time on a bunch of dick pics and shady first dates just to see if there might be something between us."

Especially when I know there's a man who can make my body sing.

A man I'm drawn to like a moth to a flame.

A man I can't stop thinking about.

How am I supposed to sit and make small-talk with some random guy, when all I can think about is Saint's hands? Saint's lips. Saint's...everything.

Impossible.

"Fair enough." She narrows her eyes on me and swishes her wine. "But why do I feel like there's something you're not telling me?"

Because there is.

I hate keeping things from Dani. We've always been completely open with each other, helping the other work through whatever bullshit life throws in our way. But Saint just feels different. It's too close. Too personal. And his job at the Hawkeye Club makes it awkward.

How do I tell her I found someone I have a connection with? Someone who makes my heart race and my mouth dry and my palms sweaty every time I'm in the same room as him. Someone who sent me into the stratosphere when we were together.

Someone who doesn't even know who I am.

2

SAINT

T he rhythmic bump of the bass reaches me the moment I step from the car. I stare up at the club and take a deep breath. It was only a matter of time before Savage called me to fire me. He and Gabe trusted me to keep Storm safe, and I didn't, not once but twice.

So, his request to see me tonight wasn't totally unexpected. I've been waiting on it all week. Every day, I came to work thinking they would call me up and end things. But it never came. Until now.

Maybe they were drawing out my torture, giving me time to consider all the destruction I caused. Storm's house is an almost total loss. The past week, they've sifted through the ashes and rubble of her life there with Angel, trying to salvage anything.

I couldn't even bear to eavesdrop when anyone at the Club was discussing the specifics. It made my gut churn and chest ache with regret.

So, I knew this was coming. Still, it hurts. And I just wish it would come after my workout.

His call couldn't have come at a worst time. Lifting weights, running, grinding it out at the gym normally helps clear my head, and I haven't spent a second the last few days not thinking about what a fucking idiot I was.

What the hell will I do without my job?

It's not a question of money really. I have some stashed away. Most of it left over from when I played. The vast majority of my checks all went home to Jamaica for Mama and everyone else. And what was left kept Jenna content, but I was careful, and what I have will more than support me for a while, until I can find another job.

Though, what the fuck will I do?

It's not like I have a lot of skills outside being huge and strong. It's served me well after the league. Working as protection and muscle paid the bills, but that was years ago. Now, I'm pushing thirty-five, and the intimidation factor may be waning. Plus, I don't know that I have the heart to threaten people anymore, let alone actually do it just for money.

There's not much else I'll qualify for though besides looking big and tough at the door of the club and to deal with assholes.

Maybe talk football. But what broadcast is going to hire a washed-up player who has been out of the spotlight for almost ten years? Nobody I know.

That's the dream job for every former player, and I would never have a chance even if I wanted it.

And, I'm not sure I want it anyway.

I like working for Savage and Gabe protecting the girls. Which is why what happened with Storm is eating at me so goddamn hard. The dancers, Storm, everyone...they rely on me to keep them safe.

They counted on me to watch her, and I let danger walk right through the damn door—twice.

Fucking stupid.

I shove open the door and slap Tubbs on the shoulder before

I make my way to the elevator. It's still early, not even six, and the place is just starting to fill up. The after-work crowd will be trickling in soon. Friday nights are always busy. I'm sure that's why Savage asked me to come before the big rush.

So he can fire me and get this done.

Like a band-aid. Rip it off. Let it sting. Move on.

The elevator doors slide open, I step inside, hit the button, and lean back against the wall as it ascends to the second floor. Every step down the short hallway to Savage's office feels like I'm the dude from *The Green Mile* making my walk toward the electric chair. I chuckle to myself. Kind of funny considering everybody's always told me that I remind them of Michael Clarke Duncan.

Savage's office door stands open, and his voice reaches me even over the music coming from downstairs. I peer in and knock on the jamb. Gabe looks over his shoulder from his seat in front of Savage's desk and tosses me a nod. Savage waves me in.

They both look friendly enough, but looks can be deceiving, especially with Gabe involved.

Savage motions to the empty chair next to Gabe. "Saint, I'm glad you could join us. Take a seat."

I lower myself down into it while both men watch me intently. "Look, guys, I know why I'm here."

To get canned.

The man who has been such an incredible boss raises a dark eyebrow. "You do?"

I sigh and run a hand over my scalp. "It doesn't take a rocket scientist to figure it out after everything that's happened."

He narrows his eyes on me, flicks them over to Gabe, then returns his focus to me. "I think you may have gotten the wrong impression about why we asked you here today."

"Well, if we're not here for you to fire me, then I'm totally confused."

Gabe barks out a laugh and shakes his head. "Definitely not going to fire you."

"The opposite, actually." Savage smirks. "We're hoping you might be willing to step up to act as head of security for all the clubs."

Huh?

I shake my head. There's no way I heard that right. "Excuse me?"

Savage grins. "I don't think I've ever seen you look so confused."

Confused is an understatement. This doesn't make any sense.

"Sorry, I just...I'm not following here. Why the hell would you want me to be the head of security with everything that's happened the last couple weeks? Besides, that's Gabe's job."

They must be out of their ever-loving minds.

Gabe turns to me. "Things have been tense lately. New players we aren't sure about."

"You mean Luca?"

He nods solemnly. "Among other considerations. Even if Luca himself isn't a direct threat, him being back in town is sure to stir up some unrest, and there are a lot of people who were affected when Dom went down. People who may still be harboring some resentment toward us but were too afraid to act out initially." His shoulders rise and fall slowly. "If they feel like Luca is tacitly in agreement with them in retaliating against us, we could be looking at some serious fucking problems."

I snort. "No shit."

Dom Abello had an empire that was practically untouchable. Until it wasn't. And his son coming back into town does not bode well for anyone. Plus, Gabe's right. Dom's death left a lot of unhappy people—like his stockpile of goons—who may be biding their time and looking for a way to come at us. Luca giving them a reason to do it would *not* be good.

"Do you really think Luca is a threat?"

Savage frowns and steeples his hands in front of his mouth. "I honestly don't know. He swears up and down that he doesn't want to cause any problems for us, but I'm sure Dom would've said the same thing."

"Probably."

Even when I moved to NOLA to play, Dom already had an iron grip on the city. If Luca is looking to reestablish that, who knows what he may be willing to do.

"Which is why we need someone who is completely dedicated to making sure all of our locations are safe. While the club here will always be our main base of operations because the offices are here, TWO is becoming more and more popular, and once THREE opens after the new year, we anticipate a surge of attention for our brand."

Gabe nods his agreement. "Attention is good for business but also bad when you're trying to stay under the radar of the potential bad guys."

I know exactly what he is saying, and it makes sense, but I'm still not following why they want me for the job. "I understand, but..." I hold my hands up, "I'm not sure why you're looking to me for this. I almost got Storm killed...twice. Once by Luca, by letting him stroll right into her office, and once by that crazy Candace chick. My track record the last couple weeks hasn't exactly been stellar."

Savage and Gabe aren't known for being very forgiving people when it comes to damage to their families and friends. In fact, they are both pretty fucking brutal when it comes to those they love. So this one-eighty from what I thought was going to happen is making my head spin.

The man sitting next to me, who could no-doubt kill me with his bare hands before I even know what's happening, reaches out and slaps me on the shoulder. "Nothing that happened to Storm is your fault. You couldn't have known Luca was sneaking around. Or that he was going to walk right into her office as a potential client."

Savage nods his agreement. "And you certainly had no reason

to suspect that Storm wouldn't be safe with Landon the other night. It isn't anyone's fault." He scowls slightly. "Except maybe Landon's for letting her walk into the house alone in the first place, but we're not looking to place blame here. That doesn't do anyone any good. Storm is safe. Angelina is safe. And even more important, Storm's happy with Landon. So even though the loss of her house is upsetting, everything ended up on a positive note."

Except for that poor, crazy woman who burned to death. But maybe he's right. Maybe I have been looking at this all wrong and letting guilt over something that I had no control over eat away at me for no reason. It's hard not to, though.

Mama raised me to take responsibility for my actions—good or bad—and also how to carry guilt for a long fucking time. Even over things maybe I shouldn't.

"We want you to oversee security for all three locations once THREE opens. But obviously start here now. We also want you to coordinate keeping an eye on Luca until we get a better handle on what's really going on there. You'll receive a raise, we'll set you up with an office here to work out of."

I practically choke as I try to swallow. "You're serious about this?"

Savage nods. "Absolutely. Are you interested?"

"Fuck yes, I'm interested. A little shocked right now, since I thought I was coming in here to get canned. I also don't get why Gabe isn't doing this."

They both chuckle, and Gabe nods. "With more locations comes more work. On top of the new club, we have all the restaurants and bars, too. I can't be in ten places at once. We need someone whose one hundred percent focus is this. You're invaluable to the business, Saint. Try not to dwell too long or hard on what happened with Storm. There are other things to concentrate on."

Like the mobster who waltzed in here making veiled threats.

"Absolutely. You have no idea how much I appreciate this, guys."

Savage grins. "I think we do. Just don't fuck it up."

CAROLINE

Dani links her arm into mine as we walk from the town car toward the club entrance. She squeezes my arm and drops the side of her head against mine. "I'm so glad you could come tonight."

Our heels click against the hard surface of the parking lot, and in the early-evening light, the building practically glows.

"Me too. It's been a long week, and I needed it."

"How's your story coming?"

I sigh and tug on the handle of the door to open it for us. "It's coming."

Bone-vibrating bass hits us as we step inside. Dawn has her leg wrapped around the pole on center stage, and she grins at us and nods.

This place has always felt like home since the minute Dani started dating Savage. That's probably weird to some people—for women to feel at home at a strip club—but it *is*. The people here. The welcoming atmosphere. Everything encourages you to come and stay a while. It was designed that way. Brilliantly.

Tubbs flashes us a smile. "Hello, ladies." He steps forward and wraps Dani in a massive bear hug, lifting her from the ground and spinning her around. "It's good to see you. You haven't been around much."

She yelps and giggles before placing a kiss on his cheek. "I know. Kennedy keeps me busy. Savage upstairs?"

He nods. "Yeah, he and Gabe are in a meeting, but they should be done soon."

"Okay, we'll be at the bar."

"Just have Byron let them know you're here. Although, knowing your husband, I'm sure he's already seen you on the cameras."

She laughs and squeezes my arm, directing me toward the bar. "I'm sure he has."

That man watches her like...well, a hawk. I don't blame him, though. After everything they've been through—Dom almost killing her, then almost losing Gabe, then the truth about Stone coming out, now this stuff with Storm—he needs to be on-guard when it comes to the people he loves.

Dani and I slide onto the stools at the nearly empty bar, and Byron nods at us from the far end were he's helping the only other customers. It's still early enough to be quiet for a Friday.

She leans in so she can be heard over the music. "So, what's going on with your story? You're not happy with it?"

"It's not that. It's just...I don't know how to explain this without sounding ungrateful. You know I've been at the *Times* basically since graduation. And they have yet to give me anything with any real meat or substance."

Dani grins and wiggles her eyebrows. "What? Stories about sex parties aren't meaty enough for you?"

"Ha. Ha. Very funny." She's been giving me shit since the night I told the girls that I managed to get Storm to go to the party with me. It's not like I could've hidden it. As soon as the story came out, they would all know I went. But I have yet to come clean with her about what happened there. "You know as well as I do that was just a fluff piece. I want to write the real stories, the kind you always worked on before you had Kennedy."

She sighs and frowns. It's a bit of a sore spot for her. She's been wanting to go back to work but Savage doesn't want to put Kennedy in daycare, so as of right now, she's still at home with her. It won't last long, though. Dani needs to be in the action, in the thick of things. Which is precisely Savage's concern.

Byron steps up to us and leans across the bar. "Good evening, ladies. Your usuals?"

We both nod, and he winks before turning back to mix up our martinis.

Dani turns to me and places her hand on my arm. "Look, Care, if you really want to move on to bigger and better stories, you have to show old Doug that you're capable of doing some real serious, hard-hitting investigations. If you're waiting for him to assign you something, you'll be in the grave before you ever get a byline on an important story. You have to be proactive with him. The only reason I was able to get onto the news desk within the first year was because I spent my own time working on stories and submitting them until he realized what I was capable of."

"So, you're calling me lazy?"

Byron slides our drinks in front of us. "Anything else I can get for you ladies?"

I scowl at her, then plaster a fake smile on for Byron. "A new best friend?"

Dani rolls her eyes and shakes her head. "We're good, Byron."

"Okay, let me know if you want something else. Savage will call down when he's done with his meeting and it's okay for you to go up."

Dani takes a sip of her drink before she turns back to me. "And no, I'm not saying you're lazy. All I'm saying is maybe you could take a little bit more initiative if you really want to be seen as something other than an obituary and entertainment writer."

I should be mad. Whether in those words or not, she is basically calling me lazy. But I'm not mad. Not really...

Because she's right.

I've been coasting at my job because it's an easy nine-to-five. I haven't exactly been striving for much else, and it's not like I have any semblance of a romantic life to interfere with my work.

The one man I've seriously been interested in the last year

doesn't even know who I am and probably never will. Even though we shared one incredible night.

So, maybe it's time I put some of that pent-up sexual energy somewhere else. Maybe into making something of my career while I try to find my happily ever after.

I raise my glass and turn to Dani as the notes of "Sail" start up.

A peek at the stage gives me a view of Dawn's long, pale legs strutting down toward the pole. The frilly black barely covers her ass, and her tits are already freed. I almost envy the girls who work here. Savage and Gabe are incredible bosses who take excellent care of them. They get to express themselves on stage pretty much however they want to. And they make really fucking good money.

The whole having to get naked and shake it in front of strangers—some of them creepers—is the only downside. That, plus my lack of any rhythm, kind of rule stripping out as a new profession if the whole reporter thing doesn't pan out.

I guess it means I better try to keep the job I have and find a way to stay happy with it.

"Well, here's to making waves. It's about time I did it." I raise my glass.

Dani smiles and clinks her glass against mine. "That's the spirit. Just try not to end up on a mobster's hit list like I did."

I take a swig and swallow down the crisp liquid. "Duly noted."

3

SAINT

Descending the stairs after my meeting with Savage and Gabe is a hell of a lot better than the elevator ride up was.

I just got a damn promotion.

I chuckle to myself as I take the last step down into the club. Dawn wraps herself around the pole in front of me and flashes me a grin and a wink as she bends back.

She's always been one of my favorites. Down to earth. Classy. Always looking out for the other girls. Just a genuinely good lady.

What the hell is she doing in a place like this?

Not that The Hawkeye Club is a bad place to work. Far from it.

It's just, some girls don't have a lot of options. Scarlett is a single mom who needed a way to support her son without a lot of job prospects. Candy is young and unsure what she wants out of life. But Dawn just seems to have something else. Some depth of knowledge. World experience. Something that shines in her eyes when she's on stage or talking to a customer.

I'd love to know her story. Find out what drives her. But like most of the girls, she doesn't talk about her past. And I don't pry. No one really does that here.

Savage and Gabe do their background checks on the girls to make sure there's nothing in their pasts that can come back to bite them and that the girls aren't doing this under duress and for the wrong reasons, but other than that, they leave everybody's past in the past as much as they can.

Something I appreciate as much as anyone.

Once Dawn's off, Candy should be up next and then Scarlett. I haven't spent much time over here at the main club, but I still learned the routines in their orders and what they need from me while they're on stage pretty damn quick. And I'm here to provide it for them.

I can't believe, I'm going to be the damn head of security.

Did Byron know about this when we spoke the other night?

I doubt it. Because if he had, and he didn't tell me and let me wallow in my misery, that would've been a pretty big dick move. And that's not like him. Not at all.

Savage and Gabe are trusting me with something huge. I'm not waiting to start. I'm going to talk to Byron and the girls right now about my new role.

I drag my eyes off Dawn and take two steps across the floor before I stop.

Dani and a very particular brunette, who has been haunting my dreams, sit at the bar with their glasses raised together. Caroline says something to Dani, who laughs. They clink their glasses, and Caroline takes a sip. Watching her throat contract as she swallows has my cock hardening against my zipper.

Christ.

We did a lot of things that night, but one fantasy I never got to fulfill was that pretty little mouth wrapped around my dick.

Caroline laughs and leans in to say something to Dani before her eyes scan the room. She raises her drink to her lips just as her gaze falls on me. The glass stills halfway up to her lips, and her eyes widen like a deer caught in headlights.

Run, Bambi. Run.

She jerks back around to face the bar so quickly, some of her drink sloshes over the side.

Looks like she's surprised to see me. Probably about as much as I am to see her here. The girls used to come in a lot, but it's certainly been a while with everything that's been going on, plus I've been over at TWO.

What amazing luck that she's here tonight.

Kismet.

Or something like that.

She leans over and says something to Dani then pushes away from the bar. I hold my ground as she darts in the opposite direction toward the bathrooms in the back hallway.

My ability to affect her wasn't just limited to the party. Maybe there is a chance for something there after all.

Damned if I'm letting her get away this time...

Dani watches her retreat then turns to enjoy the main stage. Her eyes meet mine, and a wide smile spreads across her face. She waves, and I nod at her before I head toward the back hallway as casually as I can.

Chances are, Caroline has not told her anything about what happened at the party. Because I'm sure if she had, I would have a blonde running up to me right now to discuss it.

The dim lights and the sounds of "The Kill" being pumped through the speakers give the back hallway an almost romantic vibe. I grin as I lean back against the wall between the men's and women's bathrooms to wait.

Caroline may have been all talk and gusto during the party, but that was when she was anonymous. When she's herself, something is preventing her from acting on whatever she feels about me.

I've been around the Hawkes a long time and seen her

enough that if she were really interested in pursuing anything publicly, she's had plenty of opportunities.

It's the anonymity. It has to be. And while the thought that she's embarrassed to be with me niggles at the back of my mind, I shouldn't jump to any conclusions. Give her the chance to come clean.

That chance is now.

The bathroom door swings open.

She steps out.

Those green eyes meet mine, and she jerks to a stop. "Shit! You scared the crap out of me."

I chuckle and push away from the wall, crossing my arms over my chest. "Sorry, Caroline, didn't mean to. It's nice to see you *again*." I emphasize the *again,* hoping she'll catch my meaning, but she just worries her lip between her teeth and nods.

"Yeah, you too, Saint. It's been a while."

No, it hasn't.

I smile and take a step closer to her. She holds her ground, but her hands vibrate in front of her. "You haven't been around the clubs much lately. Is everything okay?"

She nods and shoves a hand back through her hair. "Yeah, I've just been busy with work, and Dani is busy with Kennedy, so it's been harder to get here."

God, she's adorable when she's flustered.

I nod and take another step toward her until I can feel the heat radiating off her body. The faint scent of honeysuckle fills my lungs, and I'm close enough that her tiny breaths of air float across the exposed skin of my arms.

"Well, I hope you're not working too hard. All work and no play and whatever that old saying is."

She laughs tightly, and her eyes dart around the hallway. At anything but me.

This woman is so wound up, she's afraid to let go. How can she be two completely different people?

Three, actually.

She's not the Caroline from the party, nor is she the Caroline who I met at the club those other times. The one who seemed so confident, so sure of herself. This Caroline is something different.

"Well, Saint, it was nice to see you, but I should really get back to Dani before she leaves for her date with Savage."

I nod and close the final gap between us. My chest practically touches hers, and I lean down until my lips brush against her ear. "It really was nice to see you, Caroline, but I have to say, I prefer you like this rather than with your beautiful face covered with a mask."

She freezes, and a gasp slips from her parted lips before her eyes dart up to meet mine. I hold her there with my stare for a second before she ducks around me and races back toward the club without a word.

Everything's out in the open now.

It's time to let Caroline know where I stand.

CAROLINE

Oh, my God. He knows.

I just about shit myself when he leaned in and whispered those words.

Did he know the whole time? Or did he just figure it out? Shit. Shit. Shit.

My heart races as I make my way across the main room back toward the bar. Dani leans across the bar-top, deep in conversation with Byron, and barely notices my approach. I scramble up onto the stool next to her and down the rest of my drink in two gulps. Her eyes widen, as do Byron's.

She sits back on her stool. "Damn, girl. Slow down. We have

at least another hour before our dinner reservation. We have all the time in the world to get toasted."

Byron chuckles. "I can make you a stronger one next time."

I shake my head. "It's not that. I'm just..."

My glance back toward the hallway is just in time to see the man in question re-appear. He flashes me those perfect white teeth in a smug smile and winks at me.

Fucking winks.

Heat radiates out through my body from my core. My pussy clearly remembers having him inside me.

"Was that for you?"

I turn back to find Dani with an eyebrow raised. She nods in the direction of Saint.

Double shit. Try to look clueless.

I shrug as nonchalantly as possible.

Byron narrows his eyes on me and raps his knuckles on the bar. "Looks to me like there's a story to tell."

He grins, and I scowl.

"Nope. No story. Just ran into him in the hallway on my way back to the bathroom."

Dani takes a sip of her drink and leans back slightly. Her eyes skim up and down my body then narrow in on me. "There's more to it. Spill."

Well, hell. What's the point in trying to keep it secret anymore?

It might actually be helpful to get some outside perspective on all this.

"I'm going to need at least two more drinks if we're going to do this."

"Say no more." Byron turns back and grabs some vodka while Dani sets down her drink and greedily rubs her hands together with glee.

"Ooo, I can already tell this is going to be good."

I scowl at my best friend. "You really love other people's discomfort, don't you?"

Her jaw drops as she feigns innocence. "What? Me? No! I can just tell something juicy is going on, and all I do is spend my time with a toddler these days. So, I need something juicy."

I snort. After everything she's told me about her and Savage's relationship...

"I'm sure Savage keeps things very juicy for you."

She wiggles her eyebrows. "You're right, but that's not what I was referring to. I meant adult interaction and stories. So spill."

I take two massive drinks of the marvelous concoction Byron made for me then meet Dani's inquisitive eyes. Byron leans against the bar, anxiously awaiting my story.

Here goes nothing.

"So, you know I went to that party with Storm a couple weeks ago to interview the owner, right?"

Dani nods, and Byron's eyebrows rise. "What party?"

I bite my lip. This is a little embarrassing. "*An Intimate Affair* party."

He barks out a laugh and rocks backward. "Damn, Caroline. I didn't think you had it in you. And Storm went with you? How the hell did you manage that?"

Crap.

It's one thing to out myself, but now, I've also outed her.

"You can't say anything to anyone about her being there."

He sobers immediately, crosses his heart, and holds his fingers up. "Scouts' honor."

I narrow my eyes on him. "You were a Boy Scout?"

His smile makes an appearance, and he shrugs. "I was the first Eagle Scout in my troop. Little did they know they had a queen in their midst. I promise I won't say anything."

The words send a warming calm over me and reduce some of the tension building in my shoulders. Byron is as trustworthy as they come. He'll keep his mouth shut.

I take another swig of my drink to try to locate some courage.

"So, at the party, it was a masquerade ball, but I saw someone we all know. He's kind of hard to miss."

Both their jaws drop, and Byron whistles. "The big guy was at the party?"

I nod. "He was, and obviously, no mask is going to hide his identity from anyone, but I thought my identity was safe. So..." I shrug as they both lean in. "I decided to partake in some activities. With a certain person we all know."

A grin spreads across Dani's lips. "Well, holy shit. You and Saint?"

I wince a little, finish my drink, and hold up my empty glass to Byron.

He laughs and takes it. "Now I understand why you needed the drinks."

Dani looks at me a little bewildered. "I didn't even know you were interested in Saint. How come you never said anything?"

I sigh and fiddle with my empty glass. "I don't know? I guess I just feel weird about it because he works for Savage and Gabe. I mean, it's not about what his job is. You know I don't care about money or anything like that. It just felt...I don't know...incestuous?"

She tips her head back and laughs so hard, she practically falls off her stool. "You want to talk incestuous? What about Gabe and Skye? Huh? He was basically raised like their brother so you being with one of their employees is nothing."

Byron sets another drink in front of me. "I have to agree with Dani on this one. There are far worse things and people for you to be dating than Saint Clarke."

"Sounds like you're talking from experience."

He raises his hand and shakes his head. "Oh, no. We're talking about you here, not me. All I'm going to say is that the last couple weeks seem to have been very eventful for a lot of people around here in the hooking up with potentially the wrong person department, but look how good everything turned out for Storm and Landon."

Yeah, who met at the same party.

I don't say that part out loud because I'm pretty sure Byron doesn't know and doesn't need to.

Dani bumps me with her knee. "So, back to you and the big guy. Was it good?"

I snort and twirl my glass between my fingers. "Good doesn't even begin to describe it. It was ethereal."

"Then, girl, I highly recommend you do it again."

If it were only that easy. I glance back in the direction where I last saw the man in question, but the coast appears clear. He must've gone to the back.

"I wish it were that easy."

She shrugs. "It is. You're both adults, and we just had this very same conversation with Storm. You were totally on board with her doing the friends with benefits thing, or something more. There's nothing stopping you."

Except my own inadequacies.

"Maybe." I shrug. "But I've just gotten done rededicating myself to my career. I don't know if I have time for something else or want it. I don't even know if we have anything in common."

Dani shrugs. "Well, you both like to fuck. Each other."

I glower at her. "That's not what I meant. I meant outside our physical attraction."

"Well, you'll never know if you don't talk to him and try to see if there's something there, right?"

True.

"Also," she leans in and so does Byron, "I've been dying to know. Is he that big everywhere?"

She raises her eyebrows, and I practically choke on my drink.

I managed to swallow and scowl at her.

"It's none of your business."

Yes. Yes, he is.

4

CAROLINE

The cursor blinks on my computer screen, taunting me with the lack of words there. I've been staring at it for what feels like forever, though it's probably only been a half an hour.

This damn article is just not coming to me. I don't have it in me to write another boring piece about a new restaurant opening.

Dani's words have been echoing through my head since Friday.

"Maybe you could take a little bit more initiative if you really want to be seen as something other than an obituary and entertainment writer."

She's right, and that knowledge, coupled with my run-in with Saint, has left me so discombobulated, it feels like I might be going certifiably insane.

He knew it was me. Or, at least, he knows now.

Whether he knew at the party or just figured it out somehow doesn't matter. What does matter is that I'm going to have to see him, knowing he's been inside me, knowing he's touched me, kissed me, knowing I have not been able to stop thinking about it.

So, work is good. It keeps my mind off of that...somewhat. I just need to be working on something else, something more fulfilling.

And my mind keeps coming back to one thing.

Well, one person.

The one who is causing so much new turmoil for the Hawkes.

Luca Abello.

But again, Dani's words from the other night have continued to echo through my head. *"Try not to end up on a mob boss' hit list."*

That warning has been the only thing preventing me from giving in to my curiosity—professional or otherwise—about the man.

If he's a danger to the Hawkes like it seems, then he would be a danger to me if I dug into him. But what if I could find something to help. Something that could bring Luca to his knees?

I pull up the main database and type in his name. The screen fills with information.

Luca Angelo Abello. DOB: June 25, 1985, New Orleans, Louisiana. Father, Domenico Francis Abello, DOB: December 3, 1955. Mother, Patricia Angelina Abello (nee Clemenza), DOB: August 23, 1960. Aliases: Luca Clemenza.

Nothing else.

Damnit.

Though, not totally surprising. This database is limited. But it doesn't mean there's nothing there.

Maybe this is it. Maybe my big story, what I should be researching, what I should be investigating...is Luca.

Dom ruled the city, and now, Luca's back to take his place. A new mobster in town, one with an unknown history because he's been in New Jersey.

Shit.

But Dani will fucking kill me if I start investigating an Abello.

Not to mention, he might. This is exactly the type of trouble she warned me not to get into, but finding out more about him could mean helping the Hawkes stay safe.

So, it's a win-win, right? I get my story and hopefully promotion, and I help my friends.

"Caroline!"

I jerk around and close my screen.

Doug stands in the doorway with his eyes narrow on me. "What are you doing? Is your story ready?"

Fuuuuckkkk.

I shake my head. "Not yet. I should have it on your desk in a couple hours."

He sighs and growls. "I really wish you would stop waiting 'til last minute with this shit, Caroline."

Strike one against me getting my promotion.

"Sorry, sir. Just polishing it up, but I'll have it to you soon."

"You better. Dani never did this shit." He mumbles something else under his breath as he walks away.

It should probably bother me to be constantly compared to Dani, but it doesn't. She's a damn good reporter, and she was fucking phenomenal at her job—something I aspire to even if only recently.

The beep of a text message coming in has me scrambling to find my phone in my purse. Unknown number.

> **When can I see you again without that mask on?** <

Holy shit. It's Saint.

Heats rushes through my body, and my heart hammers in my chest as I stare at his words. He wants to see me. I guess it shouldn't be a surprise after our interaction in the hallway Friday night. But I haven't had a chance to prepare myself to really think through what pursuing something with him would mean.

But, maybe that's the problem.

Maybe I shouldn't be thinking it through at all. Maybe I

should just be acting on impulse. Going with the flow and what works for the now. The rest will come later.

My hand shakes as I write my response.

< **When do you want to see me?** >

That was good, right? Smooth and not desperate?

Because I'm not desperate. Not really. It wouldn't be hard to go out to a bar and find some random guy to go home with if that's what I really wanted, but it's not what I want and hasn't been for some time. I just never thought Saint would be an option, but now that it's there, and being dangled right in front of me—again—how can I possibly say no?

The three little dots appear letting me know he's responding, and I hold my breath.

> **Tonight? My place.** <

Tonight? His place? Holy shit. Am I ready for this?

It's time to put my big girl panties on. Or take them off, as it may be. I suck in a deep breath and reply.

< **Yes. What time?** >

> **Seven. 8115 Maple Street.** <

That's it. No other directions. No other comments.

What is tonight? A date? A booty call? I mean, what the fuck?

I need some major girl advice here. And there's only one person I can call. I tap my finger against the desk as I wait for her to pick up.

"Hey, how are you, girl?" Dani sounds out of breath. No doubt chasing Kennedy around.

"Saint just invited me over to his place tonight." And I have no fucking clue what to do with that invitation.

She squeals so loud, I have to pull my phone away from my ear. "Woohoo. You want it right?"

"Well, yeah, but I have no idea what to expect."

Am I walking in to something romantic?

Something sensual?

Are we going to talk?

Are we just going to fuck?

She sighs. "Don't go in with any expectations. Just go."

"I can't just go."

"Why the hell not?"

Isn't it obvious?

"Because what if it's a booty call and I go over there in fucking sweatpants and a T-shirt."

Dani barks out a laugh, and Kennedy giggles in the background. Savage's low voice rumbles something. "Savage says hi. Look, if you want to have sex with him, go over there just for sex. If you don't want to have sex, go over there not just for sex. Although, sometimes that backfires when you wear granny panties. Anyway, just stop worrying too much about it and just do it."

"Gee. Thanks for the sage advice."

Not.

That has to be the least helpful thing Dani has never said to me. Here I thought her experience in all things sex would assist.

"Anytime. I have to go. You better call me A.S.A.P. tomorrow and give me all the deets."

The line goes dead, and I sit and stare at the top of my desk in a daze. Today is truly going to be one of big changes—in all aspects of my life.

Am I ready?

SAINT

Another check of the condo garners the same results as the last dozen times. Everything is clean. Everything is in its place.

I tend to run a tight ship, but knowing Caroline will be here in just a few moments has had me on edge all afternoon. For such a tiny woman, she sure has a tremendous ability to throw me off axis.

Calm the hell down.

Easier said than done. The first time she stepped through the door into TWO, right after Savage and Gabe hired me, it was like an electric spark that shot straight to my heart.

She was always unattainable. At least, I thought...

But she's coming, and boy, do I have plans for us. Things we didn't have the time or ability to do at the party. Things I've been dreaming about. Things I need to help release some of the tension that's been building with everything that's been happening. Relieve some of the guilt my conversation with Savage and Gabe should have helped eliminate.

They're being generous in dismissing my culpability. The fact is, Luca never would've made it into Storm's office if I had been on her the way I should have, and Candace never would have been in her house if I had stayed vigilant. Even if I thought she should have been safe both places and with Landon, that's irrelevant. I didn't do my job.

It won't happen again.

Now that I'm officially head of security for the Hawkeye organization, I'm going to ensure that everyone—whether employee, family member, or otherwise—is protected from anything and everything. And with Luca still lurking around, the very real threat is still out there.

It will be nice to not think about that for one night. To indulge and lose myself in the woman who's been so central to my life without even knowing it.

The buzzer sends my heart racing more than any play on the field ever did. A three-hundred-pound lineman charging at me has nothing on this pixie of a woman. I buzz her in, pull open the door, and lean against the jamb to wait for her.

That little light on the elevator numbers goes up one by one. When it hits three, my breath hitches and the doors open.

Caroline steps out in a long black trench coat and heels that scream *fuck me.*

Holy hell.

I suck in a deep breath and whistle low. Her eyes meet mine, a blush rushes across her cheeks, and she steps from the elevator. She dips her head down and lets her hair fall over her face as she slowly approaches me.

Her head tilts back up, and she has that damn bottom lip pulled between her teeth.

Christ.

Her mouth tasted so damn sweet, like goddamn white chocolate and peppermint, and all I want is to taste that again. To have her lips on mine, her tongue tangled in my mouth, her tiny little hands and nails digging in the back of my neck and my shoulders.

My cock hardens in my jeans, and I grunt and shift up off the jamb as she reaches the door. Those green eyes meet mine from behind impossibly long, thick black lashes, and she offers a hesitant smile.

"Hi."

I flash her the grin that typically wins me a lot of points with members of the fairer sex and step back to invite her in. "I'm so glad you could come."

Her steps falter slightly, and I grab her arm to steady her. She glances over her shoulder sheepishly. "Thank you. Sorry, I'm such a klutz. I shouldn't even bother wearing heels."

I lean in and brush my lips against her ear. "You did pretty damn well in heels the other night."

The metal spikes digging into my lower back. The way she bent over that bed and they put her at just the perfect height for me to pound into her from behind. She did more than good. She was fucking magnificent.

But if I let the memory of that night occupy my mind right

now, I'll have her bent over the couch in two seconds instead of serving her the dinner I planned.

"Can I take your jacket?" I brush my hand along her arm.

She shivers and averts her eyes. "No, I think I'll keep it on."

"Okay."

Odd. It's not cold in here.

That hesitance is showing again. So unlike the Caroline from the party, but just as beautiful and enchanting.

She finally glances over her shoulder at me. "What's smells so good?"

I smile and nod toward the kitchen. "I'm cooking. Have you eaten? I probably should have told you in the text that I planned to cook."

Her eyebrows rise in an almost comical way.

I can't help but chuckle. "Well, I'm starving. I don't know about you."

A pink blush spreads over her cheeks again, and she shakes her head. "I haven't eaten yet."

I lean down to her again. There's no getting close enough to Caroline. "I hope you like spicy."

Because I sure as fuck do.

She nods and pulls that lip between her teeth again. "Yeah, I like spicy."

My cock throbs, and I turn from her to hide my reaction to her words. "Good, come on in."

The *click click* of her heels against the concrete floors echo through the condo as she follows me across the living room into the kitchen.

I point toward one of the stools at the island. "Take a seat."

She nods and slides up onto it, revealing her impossibly long and naked legs. How someone so short can have legs that seem to go on for miles is beyond me, but I would give anything to run my hands up and down their smooth skin and to move between them...

"So, what are you making?" She nods toward the stove where I stand.

"Curried chicken."

Her eyes roll up in her head, and her tongue snakes out over her bottom lip. "Mmm."

The noise deep in her throat sends my cock to attention again. I can't even be in the same room with this woman without getting hard.

She leans forward against the counter and rests her face in her hand. "What's in it?"

"Chicken, potatoes, curry powder..." I pause, "and a few other things." I intentionally leave out the two scotch bonnets. People hear that and freak out and won't even touch Jamaican food half the time. "What can I get you to drink? Wine? Water?"

That lip disappears under her teeth for a second. "Uh, wine would be great. To be honest, I could really use a little alcohol right now."

I chuckle at her admission. She's nervous, and God, that is so fucking cute. The anonymity of the party made her feel safe, like she could do whatever she wanted without any sort of repercussion, but seeing her this way—so exposed, so one hundred percent herself—is so much better.

Intoxicating really.

The cool air from the fridge helps momentarily cool my libido as I grab the bottle of white wine. I pop the cork, pour her a glass, and set it in front of her.

She raises an eyebrow. "You're not having any?"

I shake my head and smile. "I don't drink."

"Oh." Her eyes widen as she looks down at the glass in front of her. "Shit. I didn't know. I don't have to have any."

My heart swells, and a warmth spreads through my body.

So sweet...

I chuckle and push the glass closer to her. "Don't worry about it. You don't have to not drink just because I have a shitty history with alcohol. It's fine. Really."

She eyes me for second before she nods and reaches out and takes a glass. "Well, if you're sure."

"I'm sure."

A tiny smile tugs at the corner of her lips as she presses them to the glass. She pulls the glass away, and her tongue snakes out to lick her lips. "Mmm. This is really good."

I need to be inside that mouth. Those lips wrapped around me, not the glass.

"Where did you learn to cook?"

I chuckle as I stir the curry. "I don't really cook. This is one of a handful of things I can manage. It's my mama's recipe. Kind of one of those meals I just always had a lot growing up in Jamaica."

Her eyes widen, and her mouth drops open. "You're from Jamaica?"

I bark out a laugh at her bewilderment. "Yep. I lived there 'til I was sixteen."

"But you don't have an accent."

Everyone comments on that. People expect me to sound like one of the guys from *Cool Runnings*.

"I know. I came here for high school, to have better opportunities to potentially get a college football scholarship. I really wanted to blend in. I did everything I could to try to lose my accent so I wouldn't get made fun of."

She frowns. "You were made fun of?"

"I was a massive black kid with an accent who came in during junior year and took the starting position from the most popular kid in school. I got a lot of shit. Mostly just jokes and rude comments. But I was so huge, nobody messed with me much."

She laughs and takes a sip of her wine. "That doesn't surprise me."

I chuckle at that and turn off the stove. "Dinner is ready."

Her eyes follow me around the kitchen as I scoop the rice

onto two plates and then cover it with the curried chicken. I set the plate in front of her, and she leans down to examine it.

"It looks good, but how spicy is it?" She raises an eyebrow.

I make my way around the counter to sit next to her on a stool. "I promise, it's not too spicy."

She offers me a tentative smile and puts the first bite into her mouth. Her eyes widen, and a low, throaty moan slips from between her lips.

"Oh, my God, Saint!"

The exact words I'm hoping to hear later.

5

CAROLINE

Oh, my God.

"This is so good!"

It's like an explosion of flavor in my mouth. There's definitely heat there, but it's not as bad as I was expecting it to be. This is better than most of what I would get in restaurants.

"This is amazing, Saint. Where did you learn to cook like this?"

He shrugs as he takes a bite from his plate. "Like I said, it was one of my grandmother's specialties."

Grandmother?

"I thought you said it was your mama's recipe?"

A low rumble of a laugh precedes his grin. "We call our grandmothers *mama* in Jamaica."

"Then what do you call your mom?"

"Mommy or mummy usually."

"Doesn't that get confusing?" I swallow another bite as the particulars of the Jamaican customs whirl through my head.

Mama? Mommy? Mummy? Too confusing for me.

"Not really. Here it would confuse everyone, though."

I laugh before taking another bite. Different flavors I can't quite place dance across my tongue. "What are the spices in this? I'm not a cook, or a baker for that matter. Or anything domestic, really, but this is so good, I'd love to be able to make it."

He flashes me that panty melting grin again. "Onion, thyme, garlic, lime juice, and scotch bonnets."

I practically choke on the bite in my mouth, and after a second of coughing and sputtering, I manage to clear my throat. "Isn't that like one of the hottest peppers in the world?"

His massive frame shakes with his laugh. "They're pretty hot, but I don't think they are the hottest in the world. We don't cut them open for this dish, so they aren't nearly as spicy. It's the seeds not the pepper itself that's hot."

That makes sense. If I had known this had scotch bonnets in it, I probably wouldn't have even tried it. Even growing up and living here, surrounded by the spices of Creole and Cajun cooking, I've never really developed the taste for anything that burns my tongue or throat.

This, however, is incredible. I take a couple more bites and watch as he digs into his plate.

Eat slow.

Buy some time.

Sitting in this condo, having this conversation about food and his grandmother is weird enough without knowing I'm almost completely naked under this jacket.

What the fuck was I thinking? Why the hell did I come over here basically naked?

This is clearly a date, not just a booty call. I can't even remember the last time I had a booty call where I also got fed a home-cooked meal by a man.

Probably never.

And I show up in lingerie.

He's going to think all I want is sex, and that couldn't be further from the truth. I want my happily ever after just like everyone else has managed to find over the last couple years.

Is that really so much to ask?

Saint finishes his plate and turns on his stool to face me. Half my meal still sits uneaten, but I suddenly have no appetite left.

At least, no appetite for food.

His large hand on the fork...his lips wrapping around it...

God, when those hands...those lips were on me...

Watching him eat has caused a slow heat and pressure to build through my body. It's like a damn rocket firing and waiting for blast-off.

His dark eyes narrow on my plate. "You didn't like it?"

"What?" I glance down at my unfinished food. "Oh, God no. I loved it, actually. I'm just not all that hungry."

The corner of his mouth ticks up, and he reaches out and slides a hand onto my exposed thigh. Bare skin against bare skin. The warmth from his massive palm sends a shiver straight to my core, and my clit throbs. I clench my legs together slightly against the sensation.

He grins and tightly squeezes my leg.

Shit. He noticed that.

"Why don't I give you a tour of the condo?"

I swallow past the sudden dryness in my throat and nod. "Yeah, that would be great."

His long fingers graze lightly all the way down my thigh as he runs them to my knee. I bite back a moan. He pulls his hand off my blazing skin, and I hold my bottom lip between my teeth to keep from begging him to put it back.

He slides from the stool and holds a hand out to me. "Come on."

I suck in a deep breath, place my hand in his, and let him tug me off the stool. My heels clicking against the shiny floor echo slightly through the expansive room. "I love these floors."

"Polished concrete. It was kind of the new thing when this building was built, and I really like how easy it is to take care of. Plus, they look really cool."

"They do look really cool."

He leads me through the open concept living room and dining area to a hallway at the back of the condo. "Guest bathroom." He waves toward an open door on the left. "Guest bedroom." He waves at a door on the right. Then we reach an open door at the end of the hall. "And the master."

A large hand presses to my lower back, and he urges me forward.

The dark gray walls and heavy, dark wood bed and furniture give the room an incredibly sexy, masculine feel.

God, the whole place smells like Saint.

Rich and spicy and something I just can't put my finger on.

I wander into the room, my heels against the floor the only sound other than our breathing. My heart thunders in my chest, and blood rushes in my ears. I twist my shaking hands together in front of me.

What now?

Saint's hand falls on my shoulder, and he gently turns me around to face him. My breath catches. Only a few inches separate us.

And my body remembers every single second. Every single touch. Every single whispered word from our night together.

And it wants more.

I want more.

SAINT

Caroline's breath hitches as she meets my eyes. The green of her irises darkens, and her eyes narrow on my lips. I reach out and take her face between my palms then tilt her head up so I can be sure I have her undivided attention.

So fucking beautiful.

I step in to her, closing the remaining distance until my body is pressed firmly against hers. "You have no God damn idea how happy I was to see you at that party."

A pink flush spreads up her neck and across her cheeks, and she tries to tuck her head down to look away from me but I hold it steady.

"Don't look away from me, Caroline. I'm offering you a compliment. Take it."

She licks her lips and closes her eyes for a second. "I'm sorry. It's just, that whole scene was a little unusual for me, and honestly, I didn't think you recognized me or knew who I was. I don't think I could've done what we did if I knew you knew who I was."

I brush my thumb across the smooth skin of her cheek. "How come? Why would that stop you?"

A little sigh escapes her lips, and she shrugs. "I don't know. You're pretty intimidating."

I toss my head back and bark out a laugh.

Holy shit.

"So you never approached me before this because you think I'm intimidating?"

Her eyes widen, and her eyebrows shoot up. She shifts slightly. "Well, yeah. I mean, look at you."

"I've looked at myself many times."

She laughs softly. "Then you know you could snap me like a twig."

I chuckle and lean forward to press my lips against hers gently. She sags against me and returns the kiss.

It's soft. Slow. Tender.

So unlike our first time together.

I pull away, leaving only a hairsbreadth between our lips.

"That doesn't mean I can't be gentle...if I want to be. Do you want me to be?"

A breathy "no" slips from her lips, and she shakes her head in my hands. "I didn't think so."

Sex at the party was anything but gentle, and she seemed to revel in it as much as I did. It doesn't mean we won't ever do slow and sweet. There's definitely a time and place for that. But right now, that's not what either of us wants.

And that makes my cock spring to attention between us.

She hums and shifts to press her stomach against it. That's the answer I was looking for. I drop my hands to her waist to the tie of the jacket, and she freezes. Her tiny hands fall onto mine and push me away.

"What's wrong?"

She pulls her bottom lip between her teeth again, and her eyes dart around the room. "Uh, I wasn't exactly sure why I was coming over here tonight, so I wasn't sure how to dress for the occasion."

I chuckle and try to move her hands away to get at the sash, but she steps back slightly. "Caroline, I'm sure whatever you're wearing is totally fine."

Another blush darkens her cheeks. "Well...that's just it. I'm pretty much not wearing anything."

Images of Caroline's naked body flash before my eyes. My cock throbs, and a groan rumbles from my throat. "Holy hell, Caroline. Take off that jacket."

She hesitates only momentarily before she slowly tugs at the ribbon of the sash. Every second I wait to see her exposed is a second too long. But she's nervous, and I don't want to scare her by pushing things too fast, too hard for her. Though she certainly had no problem with that the other night. This is a different situation. She doesn't have the cloak of the mask or the illusion of anonymity here.

This is Caroline Brooks and Saint Clarke.

The ends of the ribbon finally drop to the sides, and she lowers her hands and lets the coat fall open.

Christ almighty.

A tiny lace thong and barely-there bra leave very little to the imagination. Smooth peachy pale skin has my fingers itching to touch it and my mouth watering to taste it.

"Take off the jacket." My voice sounds even deeper and huskier than usual to my own ears.

She nods and pulls back the shoulders with shaky hands. It slides off her arms and pools at her feet on the floor. Under the soft overhead lights in the room, she practically glows. The soft blonde highlights in her brunette hair shimmer against the paleness of her skin.

Beautiful and fucking flawless.

"Jesus, Caroline, do you have any idea how beautiful you are?"

Stunning.

Her head dips down. She's really not very good at taking compliments. We're going to have to change that.

I step forward and lift her chin with one finger. "Say thank you when someone offers you a compliment, Caroline. Don't hide. Especially from me."

She nods almost imperceptibly. "Thank you, Saint."

My name from her lips has me practically coming on the spot. It's the sweetest sound I've ever heard, next to her screaming for more while I pounded into her during our night together.

But that wasn't *us.* Not really. Those were two people pretending to be someone else. Pretending to be no one.

This is different. This is *real.*

I slip my fingers into the waistband of her thong and slowly drag it off her hips and down her legs, letting my fingertips brush along her silky skin and leaving goosebumps. She shivers and reaches out to steady herself with her hands on my shoulders.

Her panties in hand, I rise up and bury my nose into them to inhale the scent of her arousal.

Fuck yes...

My mouth waters. Her eyes bulge out of her head, and she practically chokes on her next breath.

I tuck the panties in my pocket and reach behind her to unhook her bra. It falls forward, freeing her perfect high, round breasts. Her pebbled nipples hardened even more, and I lick my lips.

"Beautiful."

She shudders at my words and shifts her hands to try to cover herself, but I push them away.

"Don't hide yourself from me, Caroline. I want to see and taste every inch of you."

Every. Single. Inch.

A low moan slips from her lips, and she sags against me. I brush the hair away from her face and tilt it up until her eyes meet mine. "Are you going to let me?"

She bites her lip again and nods. "Yes."

"Good. Now let me properly start with that pretty cunt of yours."

6

CAROLINE

God, yes.

I want to scream it at the top of my lungs and sit on Saint's goddamn face, but Mom taught me to be a lady. And at least in some respects, I listen to her. I may talk a big game, but when it comes down to it, when it comes to Saint, it's like I clam up.

And he's noticed. He keeps correcting me when I try to hide my reactions or avoid his compliments.

Compliments have always made me feel uncomfortable, and coming from a man like Saint, they are almost as intimidating as him. But I don't know why. He's done absolutely nothing to suggest he's not a kind and caring man who looks out for his friends and who wants nothing more than to please me and give me pleasure.

It's just him—his size, his presence, his...everything.

A low growl rumbles from his chest, and he scoops me up in his arms like I weigh nothing and walks me over to the bed. I wrap my arms around his neck as his mouth finds mine.

His lips mold to mine with an almost heart-stopping passion. I dig my nails into the hard muscles of his shoulders to keep myself steady as he lowers us to the bed.

I sink into the mattress, and he hovers over me on his elbow. His substantial weight would crush me if he wasn't careful, and he knows it. His tongue snakes into my mouth, demanding and taking and laying claim to something I didn't even know he wanted but I'm more than happy to give him.

Then his lips are gone from mine and are making their way down my neck and across my breasts. He sucks one of my aching nipples into his mouth, and I arch off the bed as mind-bending pleasure shoots straight to my core. Right where I want him.

His mouth.

His cock.

All of him.

Everything.

He releases my nipple and then focuses his attention on its aching twin. I roll my hips against his rock-hard cock.

Yes. That. Inside me.

I want to plead. I want to beg.

But something about letting Saint take the wheel just feels so right.

This man knows what he's doing.

He releases my nipple and pulls back and off the bed. The loss of his touch and his heat sends a shiver through me, and I push up onto my elbows.

"What? Where are you going?"

He chuckles and reaches down to grab the hem of his T-shirt. Watching him drag it up and off over his shoulders is like watching a god undress. Nothing but hard bulging muscles and dark flawless skin.

My mouth waters to lick every inch of him. Including the massive thing between his legs.

He reaches down and unbuckles his belt. The slow drag of it

through the loops is deliberate and designed to make me squirm. I press my legs together against the throb of need he's managed to ignite but hasn't even begun to satisfy yet. He knows exactly what he's doing, and he relishes it. I can see it in his satisfied grin as he pushes his pants down and releases his cock. It springs up and out toward me.

Jesus.

I knew he was big. I felt it our first night together and for days after, but seeing him in the full light in all his glory is something else altogether.

His large hands wrap around my ankles, and he drags me to the edge of the bed. He drops to his knees. "You better hold on tight, Bambi."

Shit. I'm in so much trouble.

Wait...Bambi?

His mouth descends on me before I even have a chance to brace myself or try to figure out the odd nickname. One of his huge palms flattens against my stomach, holding me in place while his lips play along the sensitive skin of my inner thighs.

Kiss.

Kiss.

Lick.

Suck.

It's everything I want and not enough at the same time. He won't move up to the apex of my thighs where I really need him.

He's toying with me.

Tormenting me.

And it is fucking delicious torture.

My nails dig farther into his shoulders, and he moans against my skin, sending a vibration up my thighs.

Fuck.

I can't take it anymore. I need his touch. I need him. "Please, Saint."

The breathy words barely make it from my lips before I whimper.

I hate to beg. I hate to show any weakness. I hate to ask for mercy, but at this point, there are more important things than maintaining some semblance of control.

He chuckles against my heated flesh—dark and knowing— and then he devours my pussy like a starving man at a damn buffet—sucking and licking and thrusting into me like he'll never get enough.

His tongue probes between my legs and shifts up over my clit, sending wave after wave of ecstasy rippling across my skin. "Oh, God."

I grip his head, the prickly, recently-shaved texture gritty against the smoothness of my palms. I score my nails across it as he lashes at my clit with a talented, expert tongue.

"Jesus Christ..."

The man isn't just a professional football player. He's a God damn Olympic medal pussy eater.

I shift and open wider for him, and he pushes my legs farther apart with his massive shoulders. A finger glides through my wetness—up and down, up and down—making me squirm and thrash against his hand holding me down.

He slips a finger into me.

Oh, my God!

I groan and clench around it, but it's not nearly enough. I want more. He drags it out slowly in time with his tongue and pushes back up into me. I arch and shift to take him deeper, and he complies, pushing into me and curling his finger up to find that magical place sure to send me flying.

"God, Saint. Yes."

He mumbles something unintelligible against my wet flesh before he pulls his finger out and returns with two, filling me completely and stretching me open, preparing me for his cock.

God, I'm so close.

My hips roll against him as he works me over. I vacillate between watching him work me over and clenching my eyes shut against the overwhelming pleasure.

"Come for me, Caroline. I want to taste you."

Jesus.

Is there anything hotter than a man saying those words to you? If there is, I sure haven't heard it.

"Yes. Yes."

He sucks my clit between his lips and pulls hard as he pumps his fingers into me over and over, harder and faster, demanding and taking, more and more.

"Yes. Yes. Yes. Fuck."

The orgasm slams into me like a hurricane crashing down against the coast. The waves of pleasure battering against the shoreline come at me from all sides as he continues to work me over. Explosions of light flash against my closed lids—streaks of lightning against a dark sky—and I arch into him until it's finally too overwhelming, and I have to push him away.

"God, stop."

He laughs and pulls away slowly, withdrawing his fingers from my still quivering pussy. I sag against the bed and look up as he rises to his feet. He towers over me—a hulk of a man with such fucking talented and gentle hands. He reaches down and wraps one around his massive cock and strokes it slowly.

I quiver and lick my lips. As much as I want this man inside me right now, I want to taste him even more.

SAINT

The taste of her release coats my tongue, and hers snakes out from between her lips as she watches me stroke my cock. I flash her a grin and chuckle. "You see something you like?"

She nods and pushes herself up until she can slide off the bed.

Holy hell.

My heart thuds, and my breath seizes in my chest. She drops to her knees in front of me.

Fuck.

I could practically come on the spot. I stop moving my hand and grip the base of my cock to keep myself from blowing my load all over her face.

I've been thinking about having her sweet mouth wrapped around me for what feels like forever, and now that it's about to happen, I barely have any control left.

Keep it together.

There's no way I'm letting this end anywhere but inside her mouth or pussy. Not after thinking about her, about this, day in and day out, since the party. Not after fantasizing about all the things we did and things I want to do to her.

I reach down my left hand and bury it into her silky hair as she settles in front of me. The hard floor can't be comfortable on her knees, but it doesn't seem to faze her. Not in the least.

Strong girl.

Despite her initial uncertainty and shyness, she's all-in now. She's more comfortable. More open. More willing to take what she wants and not second-guess herself or us. It's all I can ask for.

She licks her lips and reaches out tentatively to wrap her hand around the base of my cock. Her fingers don't even meet, and I bite back a chuckle.

Sometimes being big has its disadvantages—this being one of them—but she charges ahead, undeterred. She leans forward to take the head of my cock in her mouth, but I tug on her hair, keeping her back.

Her evergreen eyes gaze up at me with a slightly confused and lost haze clouding them.

I grin down at her. "I've been dreaming about this for a long time, Bambi. I'm not going to last long with your sweet mouth around me."

She moans, and I release some of the tension to let her shift forward and engulf the head of my cock with her hot mouth.

Sweet fuck.

I dig both hands into her hair, and she hums and slides her tongue along the underside of my dick. My legs shake. She sucks in a deep breath and takes me even deeper.

Halfway.

My entire body quivers.

Two thirds.

I grip her hair so tightly, I'm afraid I'll yank it out. I force myself to loosen my hold as she finally gets as far as she can with the head of my cock down her throat. She moans, and the vibration rushes straight to my balls.

"Fuck, Caroline."

She hums her response and strokes the exposed base of my cock with her hand as she twists up and moves back until just the head is still in her mouth. She sucks me down again with a rotation of her wrist and starts working me up toward what's going to be an explosive release.

I can't stay still anymore.

It's physically impossible.

Any semblance of control is long gone and won't be returning.

I thrust my hips in time with her movements, sending my length even deeper into her throat, but she doesn't object. She doesn't pull away. She just lets me fuck her mouth harder and go deeper until the base of my spine starts to tingle.

"Caroline." I barely manage her name through gritted teeth. "I'm gonna come."

Her only response is a low, throaty moan and to redouble her efforts on my dick. With one final flick of her tongue over the head, heat explodes through my body, and the fucking world disappears in an eruption of heat and light.

I shoot my load down her throat. Every fiber of my being sings. I tug on her hair, holding her in place as I empty every last drop. She moans until I finally sag and release her hair.

She sits back on her heels and releases my cock from her mouth with a wet pop. Those hazy green eyes stare up at me from the ground, and a tiny pleased smile plays on her lips. I reach down and drag her up against my body—my semi-hard cock pressed between us—and kiss her.

The salty tang of my release coats her tongue. It mixes with the tang of her release still lingering in my mouth to create the best flavor I've ever experienced.

This woman is something else. And she needs to know how special she really is.

I slide a hand down between us and slip two fingers into her dripping pussy. She clenches her thighs around me and moans, grinding her hips against my hand.

"Saint..."

"You want me here?" I curl my finger, and she whimpers. "You want it?"

She nods and clutches on my finger in response.

"You sure you're ready for all this?"

A tiny gasp precedes her whispered words. "More than ready."

So am I.

"That's exactly what I want to hear, Bambi." I walk her backward toward the bed and lay her down. She stares up at me with wide, expectant eyes, her glorious creamy skin so stark against the dark bedspread. "I was tested before the party, and I'm clean and haven't been with anyone since."

She nods. "Me too, and I'm on birth control."

"Do I need a condom?"

She shakes her head. "No. I trust you, Saint."

My heart swells with her words. I can't even trust myself lately with everything that's been going on. I'm surprised by how much Caroline's faith in me matters.

I grab my already hard cock and give it one long stroke as I set my sights on the glistening slit between her legs. "You sure?"

She nods and motions for me to come down to her. "I'm waiting, Saint."

7

CAROLINE

Saint releases his cock and reaches down to move me to the edge of the bed. The silky comforter under me glides across my hyper-sensitive skin. He slips a hand under me to angle my hips up then guides the head of his cock to my core. He brushes it up over my clit, sending hot fingers of pleasure clawing through my body.

I bite my lip to keep from begging again.

This man is totally wrecking me. I thought he did at the party, but this is so different. So much more. So different from what I expected tonight to be.

This isn't just sex. This is a connection. The one I'd hoped was there. The one I've been terrified *is* there.

What do we do after this?

His dark eyes lock with mine. Gold and amber flecks glow in their depths. "You okay?"

I've always overthought things. Second-guessed myself. Wondered if I was making the right decisions. I thought I was being careful and keeping myself safe. What I have really been

doing is shutting myself off from what being fun and sponta-
neous can mean.

*Don't think about all that now. Just live in the moment. Feel. Let
him blow your fucking mind.*

I nod and shift my hips, pushing just the head of his cock
inside me. "Perfect."

A grin spreads across his lips as he slowly sinks into me.

"Oh, God."

He drops his head back, and I shift my hips to try to open
wider for him. He stills. "You okay, Bambi?"

I nod and suck in a breath as he pushes deeper until he's
seated fully inside me. I clench around him, and a low groan slips
from his mouth.

"So fucking hot and tight. Like fucking heaven." His fingers
dig into my hip, and he pulls out, then pushes back into me again
slowly.

Holy fuck. Definitely heaven.

The large ridge on the head of his cock drags against my G-
spot with every thrust and retreat. He moves his hand up until his
thumb finds my clit. He rolls it in tight, small circles as he drives
into me slowly and methodically.

He's just getting warmed up, but Christ, I want him to move. I
reach up and grab his forearm. "Saint. Go."

His brown eyes darken to almost black, and a grin spreads
across his lips. "If you're ready, Bambi."

"Christ, yes."

*And I'm going to ask him what the damn Bambi thing is all
about.*

He pulls back and slams into me hard, rocking me up and
back on the bed.

Fuck!

I grip his forearm with one hand and the sheet with the other
and hook my heels around his back. He pulls his hand out from
under me and digs his fingers into my other hip before angling

me up in a way that has the head of his cock hitting just the right spot.

"Oh, God. Yes. Just like that."

Every roll and snap of his hips drives me higher and closer to another earth-shattering orgasm. My vision darkens around the edges as pleasure courses through me, and I clench him on every one of his retreats. He hisses and pushes me harder, demanding I accept more.

The slow burn of an impending orgasm spreads through my body, and just when I'm about to break, he stills.

"No!" My eyes fly open and meet his.

He releases my hips and steps back. "On your knees."

"Yes. Fuck yes." I comply and present my ass to him, throwing in a wiggle.

He steps up to the edge of the bed and wastes no time driving back into me.

Fuck. He's even bigger this way.

Every inch. Every ripple. Every drag of the head. Every time it slams into my G-spot. It's all too much.

He grips my hips to hold me steady as he pounds into me. His lips find the back of my neck, and he bites down.

"Oh, God."

His hand slips down between my ass cheeks, toward the place no man has gone before. I should be worried, but I trust Saint. A finger probes me and slowly slips inside.

Sweet mother of God...

It's just what I need to send me crashing over the cliff into ecstasy. My limbs tremble, and I gasp as the tidal wave of pleasure drags me under.

Saint drives me forward with every thrust, and I arch back to meet him and roll my hips. He leans over me and drops his hands on either side of me. He plunges into me hard and deep before he roars.

"Caroline!"

He empties himself inside me with four hard thrusts. I collapse onto the bed, and he follows, his cock still buried inside me. He catches himself on his forearm before he rolls to the side, taking me with him.

My chest heaves, and his does too, pushing against my back. His huge arms cocoon me, and I sigh and relax into his embrace.

Warm breath flutters against my neck behind my ear, and he presses his lips there gently. "Jesus, Caroline. You might be the death of me."

The death of him?

He has it backward. Saint is nothing I expected.

I guess not all saints are squeaky clean.

SAINT

Caroline stirs in front of me, reawakening my partially hard cock still buried inside her. I squeeze her gently. "You okay?"

She nods and rolls to her side, and my dick slips out of her. We both groan and laugh.

"Yeah, just starving all of a sudden."

We certainly could have worked up an appetite, though I ate enough that I'm still good. I chuckle and press a kiss to her temple. "Want to jump in the shower, and I'll go reheat more of the curry if you liked it?"

She grins. "That sounds awesome."

I slide from the bed and point toward the door to the bathroom. "There are clean towels in the cabinet to the left of the sink. Let me know if you need anything."

The smile she gives me as she stretches and snuggles deeper under the covers has my cock rising to full attention.

Down boy. Give her a break.

There's a fifty-fifty chance she's going to fall back asleep, but I have no problem with that. That woman can stay in my bed as long as she wants.

I grab a pair of boxers from the drawer and step into them before I make my way to the kitchen. The water kicks on in the bathroom. She must have decided to get up. I chuckle as I wash my hands and then make her a new plate and pop it in the microwave.

She did well tonight. I can be a little demanding, and I wasn't sure she'd be up for it outside the atmosphere of the party.

I'm so fucking thrilled she is.

There's just something about Caroline that grabs me deep in my soul and won't release me. What happened at the party only solidified that she's something special. I don't want to do anything to scare her or push her away. Not when I finally have her.

I grab a bottle of water, the plate from the microwave, and climb onto a stool to wait for her.

The water shuts off.

Huh.

That might be the quickest shower I've ever seen a woman take in my entire life. She must really be hungry. I chuckle to myself. I guess she liked the curry.

She appears in the end of the hallway in one of my T-shirts that's so big, it hits her at the knee. She shrugs. "I hope you don't mind. I don't really have clothes."

My laugh booms around the room, and I slide from the stool to make my way over to her and pull her into my arms. I kiss her gently and brush my thumb over her swollen lips. "I don't mind at all. You can take anything you want from me."

Even my heart.

I hadn't realized how much I miss this, miss having somebody to care for, to look after, having someone here when I'm not one hundred percent, when I need someone to ground me. I've always been the protector—other kids growing up, playmates on the field, the dancers at the club. This thing with Storm and everything that's happened the last few weeks has really thrown me more than I care to admit.

And now that I'm in this new role, it's even more worry and stress than I had before. They've entrusted me not to fuck up again, not to let anyone else get hurt, and that's asking a lot with a guy like Luca back in town.

Vigilance is key. So is being proactive.

I'm not going to sit back and wait until he threatens those who matter to me, especially now that Caroline and I are together...or at least, I hope that's what this means. She's part of the Hawke family too, which makes her a target just as much as anyone with the actual name.

But I have to push that out of my head, or I'll worry about it all night and not be able to enjoy the time I have with her.

I kiss her again. "I have a plate ready for you."

She glances around me at the counter and smiles. "Good. I really am starving."

My large hand engulfs hers, and I tug her toward the kitchen, but she pulls me to a stop halfway across the living room and stares at the plaques and awards on the wall to her right.

Her eyes narrow. "Who is Solomon Clarke?"

I bark out a laugh and press a kiss to the top of her head. "I am, darlin'."

She jerks around and looks up at me. "What? I thought your name was Saint?"

I shrug. "That's just what people call me. My real name is Solomon."

Her jaw drops, and she slaps her hand over her eyes. "Oh, my God. I just slept with a guy and I didn't even know his name?"

"Actually," I chuckle and drag her toward the kitchen, "you slept with me *again* and didn't know my name."

"Jesus, that makes me feel like a real asshole."

I laugh again as she climbs onto the stool in front of the plate

I made for her. "You're not an asshole at all. I don't think most people know my real name."

"So where did Saint come from? Because you played for the Saints?"

I shake my head and lean against the counter across from her. "No. That's what everybody assumes, though. I've had the nickname pretty much as long as I can remember."

She digs into her plate but keeps her attention focused on me.

"My parents were very religious Baptists, and my mother was constantly making me skip playing with my friends and going to parties and things like that to attend church functions. I'd be out playing in the streets, and she'd come tell me I needed to go home to pray." I shrug. "I was also always bigger than the rest of the kids, so I ended up protecting them from bullies on a fairly regular basis. So, they started calling me Saint."

She swallows the bite in her mouth and nods. "And it stuck?"

I nod. "I moved here when I was sixteen with my mother, and we lived with my aunt in Florida. I played football in high school, and as a linebacker, my job was to protect the quarterback, so yeah, the name kind of stuck."

"Wow." She leans forward, takes a bite, and moans when she closes her mouth around the fork. "This is just as good reheated."

I grin. "I know. I make a big batch of it, and it will last me a couple days. It's one of my favorites."

One of her slim eyebrows rises. "Will you give me the recipe or show me how to make it?"

Warmth spreads through my chest.

She wants to spend more time with me.

Not something I'm going to say no to.

"I told you, I'm not a really good cook, but I can show you this."

She grins. "You're a better cook than I am. I pretty much burn water when I try to boil it for pasta."

I laugh and make my way to stand behind her at the stool. I

wrap my arms around her and press a kiss to the side of her head. "Well, I'll teach you everything I know. Even if it isn't much."

"Awesome. So..." she pushes the food around on her plate, "speaking of nicknames. What's with *Bambi*?"

I nip at her ear before I slide onto the stool next to her. Her eyes follow me as she waits for my response.

Sure hope she finds the humor in this.

"You bolted from me after the party, and when you saw me at the club the other night, you looked like a deer in the headlights and took off for the bathroom like you were looking for somewhere to hide. So...Bambi."

She snort-laughs and nods. "Fair. I did run. Multiple times."

"But you're done running...right?"

Please say yes.

A tiny smile tugs at the corner of her lips. "Yeah, Saint. I'm done."

8

CAROLINE

I shift in my chair and can still feel Saint's cock inside me from last night. That dull, pleasant ache when your body has been used so thoroughly has been with me all day and probably will be for days to come. But I'm not complaining.

Fuck no.

Last night was incredible, and this morning...

That man knows his way around my body. Although, I don't want to know how he got so talented. I'll just sit back and take advantage of it while I can. And hopefully, while I can is a long, long time.

The way he was talking and acting last night certainly seems to suggest he's looking for something more than just a regular hook-up, that he felt that same connection I did, but I guess maybe I should've gotten that clarification before I jumped right back in the bed with him.

I'm just a sucker when it comes to Saint, or should I say Solomon, Clarke. I still feel like such an asshole for not knowing that wasn't his real name. I wanted to just crawl into a hole and die, but he wouldn't let me feel bad about it last night, so I will try not to today.

Work.

That's what I'll concentrate on.

But the blank document on my computer screen and blinking cursor taunt me...again.

Asshole.

It's been hours, and I have *nothing.* Scouring the web and all my other resources for information I might be able to use for a story, something that will bring Luca to his knees and ensure all of us will be safe, has given me diddly squat.

Luca is very good at hiding his criminal activities and keeping his personal life personal. No media coverage except a few mentions in relation to "ties" to the New Jersey mob. An occasional photo here and there from some public event.

How is it possible someone who does so much dirty work keeps themselves squeaky clean?

My email dings.

Yes!

The criminal record check I requested on Luca is finally here. I click open the attachment and scan the contents.

Holy shit.

"What?" I lean in to my screen to make sure I'm reading this properly.

Luca was arrested in Baltimore...only a few weeks before he showed up here.

For first degree assault.

My heart thunders.

This could be it.

A man with such a damn clean image and record suddenly getting arrested for a violent crime? Intriguing to say the least.

I have to find out what happened.

Every fucking detail.

I grab my phone and look up the number for the Baltimore

Police Department. Every ring tightens a band around my chest. I need this so badly. I need *something.*

"Hello, Baltimore Police Department."

"Yes, hello. Can I have the records department, please?"

"One moment."

I tap my pen against the desk as I wait for them to pick up. This is the most tedious part of my job, and something I should hand off to one of the assistants under normal circumstances. But this story is on the down-low. Doug would kill me if he knew I was spending work hours on a story he didn't assign, one that may never amount to anything.

"Records. How can I help you?"

"Hello, I'm a reporter for the *Times* in New Orleans. I'm trying to locate police reports or any other records relating to an arrest there in Baltimore. The arrestee's name is Luca Angelo Abello. DOB June 25, 1985. The date of arrest is July 14th of this year."

Shuffling papers crackle through the phone. "All right. I wrote it down. I'll have to take a look and get back with you."

"When will that be? This is an emergency."

The clerk releases a loud, long sigh. "Let me place you on hold."

Yes.

Elevator music fills my ears, and I return to tapping my pen for what feels like an hour.

"Ma'am, I was able to locate the information on the arrest you requested. Unfortunately, I can't provide you copies of these reports or give you any information from them. It is still an open investigation."

"What? But that was months ago. How can it still be an open investigation?"

"I don't know, ma'am, but we're not allowed to provide copies of reports on open investigations."

Son of a bitch.

"There's no way around this regulation? Can I get a court order?"

That would be a little extreme, but if that's what it takes to get the information, I'd be willing to file it.

She sighs. "Yes, ma'am. You can try to get a court order to have them released, but in my five years of working here, I've never seen anyone succeed in that endeavor just for an article. Not when charges are pending."

Son of a bitch...again.

"Can you at least provide me the names of the officers who were involved in the investigation?"

"I'm sorry, ma'am, that information is confidential as well."

Of course, it is. "You've been very helpful today."

"Sorry, ma'am. I'm just doing my job."

She is, but that doesn't make it any less frustrating. "Thank you."

I hang up and run my hands back through my hair. So far, this bright idea to investigate Luca has gotten me nowhere but frustrated.

The man has secrets. We all do. And secrets he wants *kept* secret are the best way to keep the peace.

So, I guess I just need to keep digging. Call anyone I can think of on the Eastern seaboard.

Luca was connected to some very important and powerful men there. The type of men who have a presence that draws attention. He's managed to lay low, but there has to be *something*.

I won't give up. Not until I've found a way to protect the Hawkes and advance my career.

Killing two birds with one stone. It can be done.

SAINT

"What were you able to find out?"

Having Savage, Stone, and Gabe all staring me down is not top on my list of pleasant things in my life. Top of that list is Caroline. This is pretty much at the bottom.

I've only been in my new job for less than a week, and already, they want information on Luca.

Like it's so fucking easy.

"It's pretty fucking hard to find anything on him, guys. I've been trying to locate info on what he's been up to. I contacted a few PI buddies I used to work with, but all I've really managed to dig up is that he's settled back in to Dom's old headquarters and is trying to rebuild some of the businesses."

Stone barks out a sardonic laugh. "I hope he enjoys the blood splatter on the wall behind the desk."

Gabe tosses him a dirty look.

Stone just shrugs. "Sorry, man, but that's a little morbid, don't you think? Setting up in an office where your father was killed?"

Savage glowers at Stone. "Maybe it's the sentimental value."

The youngest Hawke snorts but doesn't say anything else while he shakes his head.

Gabe leans forward in his chair toward me. "What about the businesses? What does he have his hands in since he's been back?"

I sigh and run through the information relayed to me earlier. "Looks like he started back with the bars, the liquor distribution, the waste management, the various construction companies that are fronts, and word is, he may be starting back up the drug running."

Stone shakes his head. "It's always been so weird to me that the mob twenty years ago never would've touched drugs, but now, it seems like all the families are starting to do it, just more on the DL. I guess when you're the head of the family, you can do whatever you want, but that never would've flown with the *Cosa Nostra*."

Savage shakes his head. "No, it wouldn't have. But that's the kind of shit we need to be worried about. That's the kind of stuff that brings danger to our front door. We all saw what happened when Dom got into the turf war with Castillo. People died. Buildings exploded. Bad shit went down."

He doesn't say more. He doesn't have to. All that was around the same time that Stone uncovered what Dom was really up to and Ben and Caleb were killed.

"So, what do you want me to do?"

The eldest Hawke leans forward. "Keep watching him. Keep someone on him. He followed Storm for weeks, maybe longer, so he can't complain about us following him. If he has a problem with it, he knows how to get in touch with us."

"And what if his way of getting in touch with you is with the gun?"

Gabe actually fucking smiles. Something pretty rare for the stoic man. "I'd love to see him try."

"Well, he managed to get to Storm. Because of me. But he won't get to anyone else. Now that we know what we're looking for, it's a lot easier to keep an eye out."

Stone nods. "Very true. And hopefully he'll slip up and give us something we can actually use against him."

I push to my feet and shake my head. "I don't think this guy slips up." I hate saying it, but it's true. "Luca is too cold, too calculating. He saw the mistakes his father made, and he's not going to repeat them. He won't open himself up to attack."

Savage nods and holds up his hands. "That may be true, but everyone has a weakness. It's just a matter of finding his. We'll figure it out. We trust you to get this done, Saint. And if you don't, we can always demote you back to the door."

He says it with a grin, but it's true. Actually, getting demoted to the door again would probably be lucky for me instead of having my ass tossed back on the street.

I don't want to go back to PI work and being the muscle. While some may not see what I'm doing here as much different, it is. This is a family. That was just work to pay the bills. Work that sometimes required me to do things not so saintly. Being the muscle meant hurting people. And for someone who spent his life protecting others, it ate away at my soul. Having to do that again would kill me.

Let's hope it never comes to that.

As long as I can keep the Hawkes safe and Luca from pounding down their doors, we should be okay.

"Anything else, guys?"

They all shake their heads, and Savage nods toward the door. "No, we have some other things to discuss, but you can go."

Good, because I have shit to do.

Starting with getting in touch with my contact who has been watching Luca today to see if there have been any changes.

Right now, it doesn't seem like just sitting back is the way to go. Maybe what needs to happen is another sit-down with the man himself. One where *I'm* involved.

Maybe he needs to see we won't be intimidated, and that if he wants to get to the Hawkes, he has to go through *me* first.

I need a plan.

Once I have one, I can refocus on the only other thing that matters—Caroline.

Her kiss. Her touch. Her screams.

I step in to my office and shut the door before I pull out my phone. I didn't want to bother her and seem obsessive this morning, so I've been holding off texting since I got here, but I need to know if I can see her tonight.

< Hey. Have plans tonight?>

Three little dots pop up as I wait for her response.

> **That depends on what you're offering.** <

A grin spreads across my face as my fingers fly over the screen.

Whatever shyness or reservations she may have had were obliterated by what happened last night.

Things are looking up where Caroline is concerned. She promised she was done running, so it's up to me to make sure she stays.

9

SAINT

Caroline stares up from where she lies panting on the mattress with a bright red flush from her breasts up to her cheeks. Green eyes flash amusement at me.

Her tongue snakes out across her bottom lip. "Damn, will this ever get old?"

I chuckle and prop myself up on my elbow next to her. "I sure as hell hope not."

She grins and buries her face against my bicep. I drop down onto my back, and she snuggles into me, laying her face against my shoulder. I wrap my arm around her.

My heart continues to race, and both of us are still struggling to regain our breath.

I press a kiss to the top of her head. "Were you as distracted at work today as I was?"

She giggles, sending soft puffs of breath across my damp, heated skin. "I'd be lying if I said I didn't think about last night a million times, but I'm right in the middle of a massive project. It's been occupying a lot of my time over the last week."

"Yeah, what's the project?"

Hell.

It's impossible to ignore the way she stiffens in my arms, and something cold that feels an awful lot like dread slithers up my spine. "Caroline? What's the project?"

She sighs and pushes up on her elbows to look at me. "Promise you won't get mad."

"Oh, Bambi, when you start like that, I can guarantee you it's something I'm probably going to get mad about. We may not know each other very well yet, but it takes a lot to get me angry. Yet those words have me halfway there without even knowing what you're gonna say."

She bites her lip and averts her eyes for a second. "Well, I'm investigating a story okay...and you probably won't like what it's about."

I raise my eyebrows. "An *exposé* on a washed-up NFL player turned bouncer who now works security at a strip club?"

Her laughter floats through the room, and she leans in to plant a kiss on my lips. "You're not washed up. You're a hell of a lot more than just a bouncer and you know it. And no, that's not what the story is about, although that might be a nice human-interest piece to consider for the future."

"I'm afraid to ask...what's the story?"

"Shit. Please don't get mad."

Come out with it already, woman...

"I'll be a lot less likely to get mad if you just come out and tell me what it is."

She sighs and shrugs. "I'm looking into Luca Abello."

"What?" I push up until I'm sitting with my back against the headboard, and she shifts back and tucks her knees under her ass.

This has to be a fucking joke. A bad one.

There's no way she's dumb enough to fall into the same trap Dani did with Dom.

A furrow settles on her brow, and she worries her lip between her teeth. "I knew you'd get mad."

"Damn right. What the hell are you doing looking into Luca? That man is beyond dangerous."

She scoffs. "You think I don't know that? That's why I'm doing this. There has to be something we can do, something we can find to use against him, something that will keep us all safe."

Shit.

I don't dare tell her I have had the same thought...and so did the Hawkes. It will only encourage this insane avenue.

"Even if that's true, why is it your job to find it? It's too dangerous."

A scowl mars her perfect lips. "Who are you to decide what's too dangerous for me? Just because we slept together a couple times, you're all of a sudden my keeper?"

I cross my arms over my chest. "No, Caroline, that's not what I'm saying, but I care about you, and I don't want anything to happen to you. We've both seen what happens when you chase down a monster."

"I could say the same for you."

"What's that supposed to mean?"

She crosses her arms over her chest too. "Well, you really expect me to believe Savage and Gabe don't have you looking into Luca too? Isn't that kind of your job now?"

Shit. She's got me there.

"Caroline, that's completely different, and you know it. I do security for a living, and—"

Her eyes widen. "And you're a man?"

I shake my head. "I didn't say that."

"No, but you were just about to."

"No, I wasn't."

A smug look overtakes her soft face. "Then what were you going to say?"

"Shit." I scrub my hands over my face. "Okay, I guess I was going to say that, but it's not about being a man or woman. I mean, Caroline, look at you. You are five-foot nothing and can't weigh more than a buck ten. I'm six-five, three-hundred something. I'm a goddamn tank. And more importantly, I know how to protect myself."

She can't possibly know about the training I've done, the martial arts and weapons I'm lethal with, about what I did after the NFL to make a living before coming to work for the Hawkes. It's not something I'm proud of, but my size was my only asset at the time.

The glare she tosses at me could break ice. "I can protect myself just fine."

I grin at her. "Okay, Bambi, whatever you say."

Her jaw drops open. "Wow. Condescending much?"

I hold up my hands. "Not trying to be condescending, I just know what can happen to a woman who is not on guard all the time, who maybe let her attention lapse for a second, someone who thinks they're prepared for anything can be blindsided and get into a lot of trouble very quickly."

"And you assume that would be me?"

"I assume anyone—male or female—is capable of getting themselves into unexpected trouble when it comes to someone like Luca. I mean, he was in New Orleans for weeks, maybe even longer, following Storm and none of us caught on to it. Savage and Gabe had no clue. I had no clue. She had no clue. He could be following one of us now, and we wouldn't even know it."

She seems to be taking everything I say the wrong way. I need her to understand what I'm getting at here, what's at the heart of my concern.

"I don't want you opening yourself up to further exposure to that asshole by doing anything stupid like digging into his past or present."

She scowls again and shakes her head. "Well, it's a good thing you don't have the right to tell me what to do then, isn't it?" A slim eyebrow raises at me, and I can't help the laugh that bubbles up. "That's not funny."

"I know it's not, but if you could see yourself right now. So beautiful, still flushed from me fucking you and gloriously naked sitting there with your arms crossed over your chest, looking all stern. It's a pretty incredible sight. My Bambi has some major attitude."

<hr>

CAROLINE

I want to be pissed at Saint's incredibly sexist comments. I want to be angry he thinks I can't take care of myself. I want to be irate he's suggesting I back off the story that could potentially make my career and help all of us.

But his concern and the way he just gave me a hell of a compliment have my body reacting as if he just caressed me again.

He really does have a way with words.

And his hands.

And his cock.

He has a way with everything. I can see myself totally falling for this man quickly if I don't guard my heart, and it's probably already too late.

"Don't look at me like that, Caroline." His voice is low and rumbles across the space between us.

"Like what?"

"Like you want to eat me. We just got done doing that. Now, we are having a serious conversation. If you continue to look at me like you want to jump me, I'm going to bend you over and fuck you again, and we're just going to have this conversation again in an hour."

I scowl at him. "I was not looking at you like I wanted to eat you."

He flashes that brilliant white smile at me. "Yes, you were."

"Arrogant much?" I raise an eyebrow at him.

"Horny much?" He raises an eyebrow right back at me.

"Touché."

I do seem to be a little minx when it comes to Saint, but I won't apologize since this man is giving me exactly what I need in my personal life. I just want to have the same happiness in my career.

Is that so much to ask?

Maybe I can make him understand.

I settle back down next to him and lean against his chest.

"I appreciate your concern for me more than I can ever express, but we're talking about my career, my life. I need to do this story. And I need to do what I can to protect the people I love, and that includes the Hawkes."

He reaches out, slides his hand through my hair, pulls my head closer to his, and drops his forehead against mine. "You have no idea how much I love and appreciate how passionately you care about your friends. They're my friends too, and I love them and want to protect them just as much as you do. In fact, they pay me to do just that. But please, I already have enough people to look out for and try to keep safe from this madman. I don't need you on his radar too."

His lips find mine with a tender, reverent kiss.

"Please, Caroline. I just found you. I don't want to lose you."

Well, damn.

When he says it like that, it's so goddamn sweet.

How can I be pissed at a man who cares that much for me and just wants to protect me?

I can't be.

But I also can't give up the story.

It's too important, and I'm too far down the rabbit hole to come back up.

What he doesn't know won't hurt him.

"I appreciate your concerns, Saint. I really do, but I'll be okay."

He takes my face in his massive hands. "Tell me you're going to drop the story."

I nod.

A little white lie. To appease the big guy.

I don't say the words, but he seems to accept my answer.

He drags me up and across his body until I'm straddling his lap. His cock stirs to life between my legs and presses against my hypersensitive clit. I roll my hips, spreading my wetness over his length. He grunts and presses his face into my neck.

"Seriously, Caroline..." he squeezes my waist, "don't do anything stupid."

I press my lips against his and take his face between my palms. "That's a promise I can make."

I don't intend to run off half-cocked after Luca Abello. I have to take things slowly and know what I'm getting into and what I have before I act.

The only way this conversation with Saint is ending is if I end it. And it needs to end now, before he asks for more commitments and promises.

I reach down between us and grasp his cock as I lever myself up. I position the head at my core and slowly sink down.

His eyes roll up in the back of his head, and he drops it against the headboard.

I'm fully seated on him, and I squeeze his hard flesh.

A litany of unintelligible curses falls from his lips.

There are two ways to distract a man—through his stomach and through his cock. I can't cook worth a shit, but one thing I do know how to do is please Saint Clarke.

10

SAINT

"Saint, I've got something for you. I'll be there in an hour."

The message came in sixty-seven minutes ago.

Michael is an incredible PI, but he's less than prompt. I stare at my desk and tap my fingers while I wait. There's not much else to do. Waiting. Waiting. And more waiting.

It seems like all I've done for the last three weeks since I got this job.

Waiting for information. Waiting for Luca to make a move. Waiting for the next moment I can take Caroline in my arms again.

The giant monitor on the wall that displays live video feeds from the two clubs and the various restaurants and bars under the Hawkeye umbrella shows there's nothing important going on that needs my attention. Two in the afternoon is too early for there to be much trouble. Things don't really start picking up until dinnertime or later.

A few of the regulars mill about at the clubs, but none of them are troublemakers, and we have great bouncers at all those locations. Which is good. It gives me time to focus on the important stuff.

And now, it looks like we've finally caught a break.

I sure hope whatever he has is good because when I think about the look in Caroline's eyes when she told me she was going to drop the investigation weeks ago, my stomach clenches along with my fist.

She was lying.

She might've thought she convinced me or that she managed to distract me by the way she rode me like a fucking cowgirl, but despite how incredible that was, she couldn't hide that look of guilt that flashed across her green irises before she sank down on my cock.

She's continued to look into Luca; there's not a doubt in my mind about that.

Being with her over the last few weeks—being so close, so intimate—while knowing she lied to my face has been agonizing, but I don't want to drive her away by coming across as overbearing.

The only way to keep her safe is to end this myself. Savage, Gabe, Stone, and hell, even Landon, would probably like it if we could keep things peaceful with Luca. I would too, but his veiled threat when he met with them doesn't sit well with anyone, and even if there were a truce, I don't think anyone would feel comfortable enough to accept it. Savage and Gabe thought they had a truce with Dom. And yet, he ended up taking out the club and Ben and Caleb with it.

There's no such thing as a truce with organized crime. That's a lesson the Hawkes learned the hard way. I don't need them to suffer that again, or put Caroline in the cross-hairs.

Footsteps thunder down the hallway, and Michael appears in my door looking frazzled.

He holds up his hands in apology. "I'm late. I'm late. I'm sorry."

With a huff, he rushes in and drops into the chair across from me.

I glance at the clock. "Only fifteen minutes. That's actually pretty early for you."

He flashes me a grin and nods. "It will be worth the wait."

"I sure as hell hope. What did you find?"

A sly grin splits his face as he leans forward and rests his elbows on his knees. "So, I've been on him for a couple days, alternating with Robert and Sammy. Well, we got together today to compare notes. Neither one of us had noted him going anywhere unusual or doing anything suspicious, but when we got down and looked at his schedule..."

"You found something?"

"Maybe. We think he has a woman somewhere."

My heart leaps into my throat, and I lean forward. "What do you mean?"

"Well, he's staying at the Ritz Carlton."

"Right, yeah." We all knew he had taken up residency there since he's been in New Orleans. He apparently isn't in any rush to find somewhere permanent to live, and I guess I wouldn't be either if I had that kind of service available to me twenty-four/seven and could afford it.

"We noticed that he's left a couple of times late at night and has been going over near Louis Armstrong Park. Always parks on the same block of Rampart. But we haven't been able to see where he goes without getting noticed. A couple of other nights, we've watched his room at the Ritz through binoculars and through the shades, we've seen him engage in some, let's just say explicit behaviors."

Well shit.

"When did he have time to find a woman while stalking Storm?"

Michael leans back with a shrug. "Who knows. Now that we've noticed a pattern, it's been tricky to find out more. He's keeping himself well-guarded at the Ritz and is careful when he's out in public. He ditched me the other day when I was following."

No surprise there.

A man like Luca has been trained to spot a tail and know how to get rid of it pretty quickly, without drawing other attention to himself. If he doesn't want to be seen, he won't be. Which is probably why he's parking on the same block and walking to wherever he needs to go. He can get lost in that area on the street with the crowd and easily shake off a tail.

"Just keep me updated with whatever you see. This could be important."

"Will do, boss. And hopefully, something I find will help."

I sure as fuck hope so.

CAROLINE

Three weeks. Three weeks of lying to Saint while spending every hour of my free time when I'm not with him trying to hunt down more information on Luca and juggling my regular assignments for the paper.

And all of it has netted me exactly nil.

I've made every call. Contacted every person I can think of, both in Baltimore and here in New Orleans, and *no one* can give me anything useful.

So, I've had to deal with the guilt about lying to Saint eating away at me for nothing, it seems.

Fucking great.

It's not like I'm asking for much. Just one little nugget of information I can use for blackmail. Not that I know anything about blackmailing someone, let alone blackmailing a mobster, but I'll figure it out when I get to that point.

If I get to that point. Right now, it seems unlikely.

"Caroline!" Doug storms in my office and slams a paper down on my desk. "What the hell is this?"

Here we go again...

The man is always annoyed or angry about something. He desperately needs to get laid. It sure has helped relax me. If it weren't for the fact that I'm lying to Saint about this story, things would be perfect between us.

"What's what?"

He scowls and crosses his arms over his chest. "The draft of your story."

I raise an eyebrow and grab the paper. "What about it?"

"It's supposed to be a light, fluffy piece about the hot new sports bar in town but you spend the entire time talking about how the waitresses are underpaid and over-sexualized. What the hell?"

I shrug and lean back in my chair. "That's just the way the story took me, sir."

"Well, make it take you another direction. If I wanted you to do serious pieces, I would assign them to you. That was more Dani's department."

Ouch.

Twist the knife into my heart a little bit more, why don't you?

The man has no concept of how insulting he can be...or how badly I want to do something that actually matters in my life.

While the last few weeks have been fruitless when it comes to Luca, they've been fantastic where Saint is concerned. The man is sweet and kind and gentle and also strong and hard and brutal. The contrast of all the things that are Saint make every moment we spend together a path of discovery of not only each other but also of myself.

He's opened me up to things I never would have thought I would enjoy. Like rougher than hell sex. And talking filthy enough to belong on late-night Cinemax.

The only problem has been knowing that I've been lying to him. Keeping what I've been doing a secret. If I really thought I were in any danger, I would've told him. I would tell him everything. But I've been careful, and I've been watching my back.

No one has been following me. There's no threat or danger here except to Luca and his hold over the Hawkes.

If I can get this story, if I can make the Hawkes safe and make a major career advance, I'll have everything I've ever wanted. My happily ever after.

Assuming Saint isn't so angry about me lying that he leaves me.

Shit.

My stomach churns at the thought, but I push it aside to deal with the here and now.

"Look Doug, if you want me to write a meaningless little story, I will, but I'm telling you right now that my days are numbered as your go-to mindless fluff girl."

He snorts and props his hands on his hips. "What? You want to be the next Dani Eriksson?"

I shrug. "Maybe? Why is that so surprising?"

"Because you don't have half the drive she does. You've got the brains and the writing chops, but I haven't seen anything from you in the years you've been here to suggest you have any desire to do anything other than write fluff." He waves his hand over the piece of paper. "Which is why I assigned this. Instead, I get a statement, which is exactly what I don't want for the story. Rewrite it and make sure it's ready to go by print."

I salute him and fight the desire to roll my eyes. "Yes, sir. Whatever you say, sir."

He glares at me, and his nostrils flare. "Lose the attitude. You may think I'm an asshole but I'm still your boss."

"I don't think you're an asshole, sir. I know you are."

He scowls and storms out of my office.

Maybe calling the boss an asshole isn't the greatest idea in the world when I want a promotion, but he was kind of being a dick, so it's not like it was a lie.

Plus, he knows he's a dick and always has. Dani called him one to his face more times than I can count. Then again, she seems to get away with that shit, probably because she looks like a damn Barbie doll and has balls bigger than most men I know.

I wish I had half of what she does.

But what I do have is determination—to get the story done and to do it without ruining what I have with Saint.

Even if that means taking a step that's more dangerous than anything Dani ever did while investigating Dom.

If things don't turn around soon, the only choice is to walk into the lion's den. Going in empty-handed, with no weapon—literally or figuratively—is stupid. I would much rather go in with a fistful of blackmail material, but if I can't find it, then a change in tactic may be in order.

It's a last resort.

One I hope I never have to take.

I'll do my due diligence before it ever comes to that.

Because that's something Saint may not be able to forgive me for.

11

SAINT

The thumping bass playing in the club almost drowns out my phone ringing, but I manage to grab it from my pocket just as I step into my office after a day of checking on the security at all the Hawkeye locations.

"Yeah, what is it? Do you have something for me?"

It's been a long month since anything new came in from the men I've had sitting on Luca. The promising information about a potential woman in his life, maybe a weakness and way to get him, has amounted to nothing, because no one has been able to find her.

Luca is one slippery fucker. He dodges tails and keeps his windows covered so the only thing visible is moving shadows. He's smart.

Too fucking smart.

His arrogance will be his undoing. He thinks he's untouchable, but he doesn't know me. He doesn't know what I will do when I'm driven and pushed. And right now, the need to get Luca out of the Hawkes' lives and out of mine is almost as strong as my need for Caroline.

I fucking love her.

But she's lying to me.

Every day, she looks me in the eye and tells me about her day at work, and I can see it. I know she's been working on the Luca story. Because some of her contacts are my contacts too, and they tell me everything relating to Luca, including who else has been asking questions.

This needs to end. And hopefully this call will do just that.

Michael clears his throat. "I don't know, sir. I think the woman we've been looking for may have just showed up at his office."

I stop next to my desk. "Do you know who she is?"

"No."

"Describe her to me."

"Tiny. Probably about five feet and a hundred pounds at best my guess. Sandy blondish maybe brunette hair. She was carrying a leather satchel over her shoulder and walked right in like she owned the place, so I don't think it was somebody he doesn't know or wasn't expecting."

Caroline. Son of a bitch.

I knew she was working her investigation, but she actually went there...actually showed up at his place.

What the fuck is she thinking?

I growl into the phone and tighten my hand around it. "How long ago was this?"

"Just a minute ago. She literally just walked in, and I called you right away."

"Good. Stay there. Call me if anyone else comes in or out. I'm on my way."

"On your way? You're coming here?"

Damn fucking right I am.

I'm not letting my woman sit in a room with that man. Even if I have to go in literally guns blazing, I'm bringing her out. Even if she's kicking and screaming. Even if it ends us. I have to protect her.

"Yes. I'll be there in half an hour, tops."

Why the fuck does it have to be so far?

I shove away from my desk and rush out the door toward the stairwell.

Gabe sticks his head out of his office. "What's going on?"

I pause for a second. "Caroline's meeting with Luca right now."

His eyes widen, and his eyebrows shoot up. "What? Are you sure?"

"Yeah, my guy sitting on Luca's place just called to tell me."

Gabe growls and steps out into the hallway. "Jesus Christ. What the fuck is she doing there?"

"I don't know, but I'm gonna go find out."

He steps toward me. "I'm coming with you."

"No." I hold up my hand to stop him and shake my head. "I got this. Just let Savage know what's going on so he can tell Dani."

Gabe nods but the anger at being told *no* clearly boils beneath the surface of his green eyes. "Call me if you need anything at all. If you need back up. And call me the second you get out of there to let me know she's okay."

I nod and charge down the steps three at a time. Blood thunders in my ears as I sprint across the parking lot toward my car.

Jesus, Caroline, what the hell were you thinking?

She's poking a damn hornet's nest.

I knew she was going be the death of me, but I never thought it would be the actual death. I was thinking more along the lines of the end of bachelorhood and my days of wandering and being lonely. The death of my ability to be with any other woman. That sort of thing.

Now we're talking bullets to the head kind of death.

Both are permanent, but the bullet one hurts a fuck of a lot more.

I slam my car into drive and tear out of the lot onto the street, squealing the tires. If any cop tries to stop me on my way over there, I'm probably going to end up charged with fleeing and eluding, but at this point, it doesn't matter. The only thing that does is getting to her and making sure she's okay.

If I have to do a little time for that, so be it. The cop will understand when we pull in and he sees where I'm going. At least, I hope so. Or maybe luck will be on my side and I'll have smooth-sailing all the way across town.

Lightning streaks across the dark sky overhead, and a crack of thunder rolls. The car shakes, and the sky opens up, dropping a deluge on the city.

Son of a bitch.

So much for luck being on my side.

CAROLINE

What the hell was I thinking?

One of Luca's goons leads me down a dark hallway toward what I can only assume is his office and my final doom.

"It seemed like a good idea at the time..."

Famous last words for a lot of people and likely for me, too.

But it's too late to turn back now, and I've run out of options. If I want not only my story but also the ability to help the Hawkes, I'm going to have to face him and talk—man to man, or man to woman, as it may be.

I was looking at this stuff the entirely wrong way.

Instead of trying to expose something about Luca, I should've been coming at it from this angle from the beginning. He's too smart to leave himself exposed, but if I can play the nice guy and befriend him in a cordial, professional manner, maybe I can get him to open up about something that *will* help.

He did approach the Hawkes as a friend and ask them to welcome him back into their fold. That tells me he wants the lines of communication open. I can be that between him and the Hawkes, and maybe we can work this all out in a way that keeps anyone from being burned—figuratively or literally.

There's been way too much of that over the last few years. Far too many people I love and care about getting hurt.

I can't watch that happen again, even if it means risking myself. So, I suck in a deep breath and allow myself to be led down the hall of doom.

The huge goon, who hasn't said a word since I walked in the front door and said I was here to see Luca, stops at the end of the hallway and knocks on a large door with his massive fist.

"Enter." The voice is deep even through solid wood, and it sends a shiver down my spine. I've never even met the man, but just knowing he's behind that door is enough to have my chest tightening and my lungs seizing.

Toughen up, Caroline. Show no fear.

Luca is the kind of man who will eat you alive if you let him. So, I can't let him.

No cracks in the armor.

Get in. Get what I need. Get out and home to Saint.

Meathead opens the door and practically shoves me through it into the office of Luca Abello.

The man himself sits behind a large wooden desk in a custom black suit that fits him like a fucking glove. It probably cost him more than my car.

He rises to his feet, straightens his tie, and buttons his suitcoat before he walks around and extends his hand to me. "Ms. Brooks. It's always so pleasant when someone so beautiful graces me with her company."

His large, warm palm and firm handshake have my knees wobbling.

Dark eyes flash with humor as he squeezes my hand. My

heart thuds against my ribcage, and I release his hand. Standing there letting him feel my palms getting sweaty and that I'm quivering doesn't exactly exude the "I'm not afraid" thing I am going for.

Luca looks to his goon standing by the open door. "You can go."

Shit.

He wants to be alone.

Is that a good sign or a bad one?

If he felt threatened, surely, he wouldn't send his muscle away, but then again, Luca is undoubtedly perfectly capable of taking care of a tiny woman himself, if need be.

The door closes behind me, and I'm left alone with the cool, calm, terrifying man I probably should have stayed a thousand miles away from.

Desperate times and all that...

Luca flashes me a grin and walks back around to sit in the giant red leather chair behind the desk. He motions toward the two chairs in front of the desk. "Please sit."

Great idea, especially since my legs are quivering so hard, I'm not sure I can remain standing.

I lower myself into the chair as I scan the room. This is where Dom died. Gabe killed him here. But Luca sits in the same place, with the sly little tilt to his lips as if it's totally normal for him to chill in the chair his father was shot in.

Well, maybe not the exact same one, but still...

What kind of sick fuck does that?

One who is currently narrowing his dark eyes on me like he knows something—maybe how fucking terrified I am and how clueless I am about how to approach this entire thing.

I thought I was prepared. The last almost two months researching him have given me a pretty good understanding of what I'm up against.

Intelligent. Conniving. Merciless.

And secretive.

Luca steeples his fingers in front of his mouth and nods. "So, it seems we have things we need to talk about, Ms. Brooks."

I swallow against the thickness in my throat and try not to fidget with the strap of my bag. "It seems so."

He watches me but doesn't say anything. A minute ticks by with nothing but silence hanging in the air around us.

Why isn't he saying anything?

I squirm a little in the chair. "Oh, you want me to go first?"

A low chuckle slips from him, and a tiny smile tugs at his lips. If I didn't know who he was and how dangerous he can be, I could see how easily he would be able to lure me into his bed.

The man is hot.

There's just no other way to say it.

The dark and mysterious thing coupled with the power he exudes is simply panty-melting.

"I think that's a good idea, Ms. Brooks, because you probably aren't going to like what I have to say."

12

CAROLINE

S *hit.*

I thought I was prepared for this when I climbed in my car and drove over here—after weeks of getting absolutely nowhere, it seemed like the only option—but apparently not.

Deep breath, Caroline. Here we go.

"All right, Luca, here's the deal. The Hawkes have been through enough because of your family, so you're going to leave them alone."

He barks out a laugh and rocks back in his chair slightly. "I made it very clear to them that I had no intention of hurting them and that I wanted us to rekindle our friendship from childhood. What makes you think I would want to cause them any further pain than what my father already did?"

"Because of who you are. Because of what you do. Nobody trusts you, including me. So, I thought having a little incentive to keep you in line may be the way to go."

His eyes narrow on me. "What is it you think you have that could incentivize me to keep my hands to myself?"

I shift nervously under his assessment and clear my throat. "I know that there are certain people in New Jersey who aren't very happy with you and that it has something to do with your assault arrest last year."

Total shot in the dark.

Really, I know nothing.

The only thing I managed to piece together was that the Baltimore arrest occurred right before he appeared here, and my sources in Jersey made it clear he's *persona non grata*.

But he doesn't know that. I might know everything. I might have a hundred sources ready to come forward on this. I might be able to blow his world wide open.

He nods his head slightly. "Even if you have the information you're insinuating, I'm still not seeing what it is you think you're going to do with this information."

"What do you think would happen here in New Orleans if everyone got wind that you had a falling out with *La Familia*?"

This may be a different city. A different state. But there's no doubt part of Luca's power here flows not only from his father's reputation, but also from his connections to one of the most powerful families in the country.

Without them, what will he have?

"What is it you think you know about my...how did you put it? Falling out? With them?"

He's calling my bluff, and I have nothing.

Shit.

"I have two police officers from Baltimore willing to talk about what you did."

Lies.

But I sit stock-straight and hold my ground.

If I don't flinch, he won't know I'm completely full of shit.

A grin spreads across his face. "I highly doubt that, Ms.

Brooks, but if you really want to know what happened, let's make a quick phone call, shall we?"

"To whom?"

He doesn't respond, just leans forward, grabs the phone on his desk, and dials a number. He presses a button on the phone, and the sound of it ringing fills the room.

"Hello?"

"Mr. Jacobson? It's Steele."

"Oh, hello, sir."

Mr. Jacobson?

Steele?

Sir?

Who the hell is this guy?

"I'm sitting here with Ms. Brooks. She's been doing some digging and is interested in my arrest at your establishment."

His establishment?

The arrest in Baltimore?

This guy must be the owner of where it happened.

"Mr. Jacobson, would it be fair to say you have never spoken to anyone about what happened? Including the police?"

The man clears his throat. "No. You told me not to talk, and I didn't."

Luca flashes a knowing grin at me over the desk. Of course, the police wouldn't talk to me. If Luca paid off the business owner, he sure as hell also paid off the cops.

"I appreciate your discretion, Mr. Jacobson, but I want you to tell Ms. Brooks who you are and what really happened that night."

"You want me to tell her everything?" The disbelief and distress in his voice flows through the line.

Whatever Luca said or did to get him to stay quiet has worked. This request has thrown him.

Luca's dark eyes meet mine across the desk, and he nods. "Yes."

The man on the phone clears his throat. "Um...I own a bar called The King's Room in Baltimore." He pauses long enough for the silence to become uncomfortable.

Luca leans toward the phone. "It's okay, Mr. Jacobson. Tell her."

A sigh slips though the line. "It's a gay bar."

Gay bar?

Luca was arrested for assault.

Holy shit! Was he gay-bashing?

It's not a surprise that a big, bad mafia guy would do something so despicable like that, but it also seems like a dumb move Luca is too smart to make.

"And...back then...Mr. Abello was a frequent flyer here. Only he went by Steele."

Frequent flyer?

The cogs in my brain turn slowly.

I got it all wrong...

He wasn't there gay-bashing...

He was there because he's *gay.*

Holy shit.

The man on the phone continues as I try to wrap my head around this.

"Steele was always looking out for the guys at the club. If someone was sketchy or something didn't feel right, he was the first one to help the bouncers get them out. That night, some guys came in and started harassing another patron, and Steele stepped in to help them. Things got a little heated, and Steele decked a guy after the asshole took a swing at him. Nothing probably would've come from it except the guy fell backward and smacked his head against the bar and knocked himself unconscious. Paramedics had to be called, and the police came, so Steele got taken in."

I move my eyes from the phone to Luca. His hard eyes remain

locked on me, watching for my reaction, but honestly, I don't know *how* to react.

This was the last thing I was expecting to find when I sat down with him today.

"Anyway, I don't know what ended up happening other than he was never charged. And he asked me to stay quiet about it. I told the police I didn't see anything, and we never saw Steele after that."

Not charged because they didn't have the evidence or not charged because he paid them off?

"Did you know who he was when he was there?" My question slips out before I realize I'm asking it.

Shit.

But Luca doesn't look mad.

He flashes another grin. "You can answer, Mr. Jacobson."

"Not at first, but someone eventually recognized him and alerted me. He never caused any trouble, so I never interfered and frankly, I'm glad he decided to leave when he did, because if people had gotten word that someone tied to the New Jersey mob was driving to Baltimore to a gay club, well, you can imagine all the trouble that might bring."

The same kind of trouble finding out your son is gay or that the man you brought into your fold to work for your mob is gay.

Jesus Christ.

It all makes sense now.

Dom sending Luca and his mother away.

Luca having to leave New Jersey and why they want nothing to do with him. The incident outed him to the organization. They wanted him gone and probably ran him out before anyone else could find out the stain he had brought on them.

Luca leans forward, and his hand hovers over the phone. "Thank you, Mr. Jacobson. I appreciate your assistance and continued discretion in this matter."

He hangs up the phone and leans back into his chair. "So, you see, Ms. Brooks, the only secret is that I prefer men over women, and the little incident that occurred at the club brought some unfortunate attention to that fact, attention from the people I worked for back home. People who are, let's just say, not so accepting of my lifestyle. It was for the best that I leave so that was a major reason I decided to come home."

"That...and to stalk Storm."

His dark eyebrows drop down as he narrows his eyes on me. "It wasn't stalking. I wanted to make sure she was okay. You weren't around back then, so you can't understand the relationship I had with the Hawkes as a child. We were friends. The best of friends."

"They don't trust you, and neither do I."

"That's fair enough." He nods and leans forward to rest his elbows on the desk. "But they can really cut with the having me followed and having me watched bullshit. I'm not doing anything they don't already know about, and nothing I'm doing will touch them. I promise. I would never do anything to hurt them."

A knock on the door has me jumping and whipping around.

Christ, I'm jumpy.

"Come in."

The goon pops his head in. "Sir, we have a rather large gentleman out here demanding to see you immediately. He says his name is Saint."

Shit. Shit. Shit.

I should've known he would find me here. He is not going to be happy.

SAINT

I've been angry before in my life. About a lot of things. Games we lost. Plays I missed. Jenna leaving me. What I let happen to

Storm. But the fact that I'm having to walk into the office of Luca Abello to save Caroline's ass has to top the list.

From the moment she lied to me about dropping the story, I knew it would eventually come to this.

She's too blinded by her need to advance at work, to make a name for herself, to see that she *doesn't* need to do this. There are a hundred other stories she could have done, a dozen different ways she could have approached her boss about it, but instead, she chose the most dangerous route.

It's so fucking Caroline.

And it's one of the reasons I love her so much.

Her passion. For me. For work. For life.

I just wish it could be passion with *reason.*

Because *this* isn't reasonable. Not in the least.

I growl at the goon as he ushers me ahead of him down the hallway toward a solitary door. He gives a quick knock then pushes it open.

Caroline sits in the chair just inside the door with a tentative, forced smile on her lips. Luca gives me a knowing grin from across the desk.

"Saint," he raises an eyebrow, "take a seat and join us, please." He motions toward the empty chair next to Caroline.

I glower at him as I lower myself into it, then flick my eyes over to Caroline. She averts her attention to something on the desk rather than look at me.

Probably wise.

Luca leans back in his chair. "I can only assume you're here for her because you've never been here before and have left the job of following me to your minions."

We're doing a bang-up job of staying inconspicuous.

He flashes me a grin. "I just got done explaining to Ms. Brooks that I'm not a threat to the Hawkes, or to her, which is exactly what I told them when we met. I understand the reluctance to believe me, but all of this," he raises his hands and sweeps them around, "is really unnecessary."

Unnecessary?

"I say it's absolutely necessary. How are we ever supposed to trust you? After what your father did and knowing what *you* did in Jersey?"

Luca steeples his fingers in front of his mouth and sucks in a deep breath through his nose. "I'm going to say what I've said at least a dozen times already. I am not my father. The man didn't even want anything to do with me. I never even spoke to him after the age of ten. At all. What he chose to do has nothing to do with me or how I run my business."

"And what about your bosses back in Jersey? The ones who trained you in this business. Aren't they going to have a say in what goes on down here?"

He glances over at Caroline. A look passes between them.

What the hell?

"Let's just say, we parted ways and came to an understanding. They will not interfere with me here, and I will not return to New Jersey."

"They let you walk away?"

It sure as hell doesn't sound like the mob I know. Caroline exchanges another look with Luca that has my blood boiling and my fists clenching.

An intimate look.

Luca gives her a little nod. "Tell him."

She turns to face me, and her green eyes shimmer with fear.

Of me?

Of him?

She swallows then reaches out and lays her hand on my arm. "They let him go because they don't want anything to do with him. They found out he's gay."

I recoil slightly and look to Luca who sits still as a statue.

He's gay?

That's absolutely the last thing I expected to come out of her mouth. Though, it does explain a lot. His insistence that Dom wanted nothing to do with him. His sudden flight from New Jersey and reappearance in New Orleans after two decades.

"Wow, I had no idea."

He shrugs slightly. "It's not information that I would call readily available. For obvious reasons, I've had to keep my life-style secret for many years. For not only my safety, but for the safety of anyone I'm involved with."

"Yeah, I can understand that. But even if what you say is true about your intent not to harm the Hawkes, the businesses and the things you are getting your hands in here are inherently violent. They are inherently things that are going to touch the city and potentially people we care about."

He frowns and nods. "That, I have no control over. But if I ever thought anything I was doing could cause harm to the Hawkes, I would ensure they were protected."

I growl at him. "That's my job."

He shrugs and gives me a little wink. "And you've been doing a bang-up job of it, Saint."

Caroline tightens her hand on my forearm before I bolt out of the chair and leap across the desk at him. "Saint, stop it. It's not worth it."

She's right. It's not. The arrogance of this fucker is enough to make me want to bash his face in.

He knows it, too. The grin playing at his mouth is evidence of that. "Now, is there anything else you wanted to discuss today? I'm a very busy man and have several appointments later to attend."

Caroline releases my arm and glances over at me. She chews on her bottom lip for a second.

The past couple months have taught me how to read this woman like a book. She has a plan. Something churning in that pretty head of hers.

Shit. I'm not going to like whatever is going to come out of her mouth.

She shifts forward on her chair toward the desk while Luca looks on expectantly. The man's smugness is infuriating, but no good will come of me initiating any violence right now.

"Well, there is one more thing. I'm hoping to ask you for a favor."

13

CAROLINE

Saint glowers, staring straight ahead at the road with his massive hands clenched around the steering wheel so hard, he may snap it in two. He hasn't said a word to me since he dragged me out of Luca's office other than to demand I get in his car and to tell me he would send somebody to get my car later.

Other than a short call where he simply said, "I got her," the big guy hasn't opened his mouth. He must have been telling someone back at the Hawkeye Club what was going on.

I was right. He's pissed. Though I can't understand why.

It's my job. That's all. This was never something personal. This wasn't about standing up to Saint or going against his wishes. It was about me, my life, my career, my friends. He should understand that. And things with Luca ended amicably. More than amicably. He can't seriously be this mad after seeing all that.

"Saint, please—"

He holds up his hand. "Don't. We're not getting into this while I'm driving."

I bite my lip and sit back in my seat to wait out the inevitable shit storm that's coming as soon as we get back to his place. He pulls in the parking structure under his building and into a spot. He throws the car into park but doesn't turn it off or move to get out.

My chest aches, and the acid in my stomach churns as I wait for him to say something.

Say something. Anything.

He scrubs his hands over his face, and when he turns to look at me, tears shimmer in his dark eyes. "Do you have any idea how fucking terrified I was?"

I reach out and lay a hand on his forearm. "I know. I'm so sorry. I never meant to—"

"You never meant to intentionally lie to me about dropping the story? You never meant to put yourself in danger? But you did. Does this," he moves his hand between us, "mean nothing to you? Is that why it's so easy for you to lie to me and put yourself at risk knowing what losing you would do to me?"

"What? No. Jesus, of course not. You mean...everything."

Somehow, I've managed to go and fall in love with Saint.

And he's right—I should *not* have lied to him.

"I'm so sorry I lied to you. At the time I said that I would drop the story, you and I weren't anything more than two people who were sleeping together. I didn't know where it was going, and I wasn't going to set aside my potential career advancement for what may just be really good sex."

Okay, mind-blowing sex...

"By the time you and I really started to getting serious, I was already neck-deep into this research and was set on pursuing it. Doing this had nothing to do with my feelings for you. I felt so guilty about lying to you this whole time."

He growls. "Then why didn't you stop? You could've told me. You could've come clean anytime."

"No." I shake my head. "I couldn't. Because then I risked losing you, and I couldn't lose you."

A long sigh slips from his lips, and he drops his head down against the steering wheel. I've never seen Saint so...discombobulated. I don't like that I was the one who did this to him. Not one bit.

He reaches down, turns off the engine, and slides from the car without another word.

Shit.

I grab my bag and scramble after him. The air on the ride up in the elevator is so thick with tension, I could cut it with a knife. Saint doesn't touch me, doesn't even look at me. Normally, he would have an arm around me or his hand on my ass. He always wants to touch me, but now, it's a wave of coldness coming from the man I want nothing more than to throw myself at.

Was the story really worth it? Was it really worth risking what I have with Saint?

Right now, it sure as hell doesn't feel like it. At the time, it did, though.

What am I going to do if I lose him? What if this is what ends us for good? God, I've been such a fool. An idiot.

The door slides open onto his floor, and he makes a silent trek to his condo. He holds the door open for me and ushers me in.

It slams closed behind me, and then I'm up against the door with his mouth and hands on me before I can even catch my breath. The strap from my bag slips from my shoulder, and it falls to the floor as I lace my arms around his neck and let him drag me up his body so I can wrap my legs around his waist.

He presses me into the door as his mouth works me over. Tongues and limbs tangle. Panting breaths mingle as he pours all of his frustration and hurt and anger and concern into the kiss in a way that sends my head spinning.

I groan against his lips, and he reaches between us to unbutton and unzip my jeans and tug them down my hips. He does the same to himself while using his massive chest to press me against the door, never taking his mouth from mine.

He's a man on a mission, determined to prove something, either to me or to himself. I'm not about to stop him.

Never.

SAINT

It struck me the moment I walked through the door.

I love her.

That isn't exactly a new revelation, but I realized I've never told her, and maybe I haven't been doing everything I need to do to actually *show* her.

The thought of losing her steals my breath, and all I want right now is to be buried inside her, to show her how much I need her. How much she means to me.

I finally free my cock and shift her up on the door to align it with her pussy. The head brushes through her wetness, and I groan.

She's ready for me.

I shove up into her in one hard thrust.

"Fuck!"

Her head drops back against the door, and she pulls her lip between her teeth. "Oh, my God, Saint."

I give her only a second to adjust before I pull back and drive up into her again.

This will not be slow and sweet.

This will not be gentle.

This is me claiming her, once and for all.

This is a statement. One I hope she gets loud and clear.

There will be no more lies. No more sneaking around. No more risking her life and my heart.

No more.

She digs her heels into my back and scratches her nails along my neck. Her gasps and moans mingle with my grunts.

"Caroline, look at me."

Her head drops forward, and her glazed eyes meet mine.

"You can't make me worry like that ever again. You need to stop with this danger shit."

I drive her up the door, and her eyes roll back in her head for a second. I pause until she reopens them.

Her lips part. "Okay."

I thought maybe she'd fight me on it, but she doesn't seem to have it in her to argue right now. All I see is acceptance. Simple acceptance and love shining back to me in her gaze that tells me she's being honest this time. She won't put me through that again. At least, not intentionally.

But Caroline Brooks will keep me on my toes for the rest of my life; I have no doubt.

I thrust into her again and again, until there is no me. There is no her. There is only us.

Her body quivers, and the door rattles in the jamb so hard, it might explode into the hallway behind her.

She clenches around me. "Saint!"

And then she gasps and clutches at me while I empty myself into her.

My heart.

My soul.

My everything.

I drop my forehead against hers. Her breath becomes mine. She presses her lips to mine in a chaste kiss.

"I love you, Caroline."

A tiny smile tilts the corner of her lips. "I love you too, Solomon Clark. Even though you're definitely no saint."

EPILOGUE

TWO MONTHS LATER

CAROLINE

Dani closes the paper and drops it on to the small table between the two chairs facing my desk. "It's a great story, Care. Really. I still want to throttle you for sneaking around and investigating Luca knowing how dangerous it could be, but I know Saint already tore you a new one for it."

I chuckle as memories of him fucking me against the door come flashing back in full color. "You could say that. But really, I know it's going to take you guys a long time, and maybe you'll never actually believe it, but I don't think Luca is a direct threat to any of you. I've now spent a good amount of time with him interviewing him for the article. And I never got any indication or feeling that he would hurt me or you. There's a lot more to the man than you even know."

It's the truth.

When I gathered up the nerve to ask Luca to agree to let me

do an interview and an article about him at the end of our tense and eye-opening meeting, I never thought he'd say yes. But the opportunity to formally introduce him to New Orleans as a legitimate businessman was too much for him to pass up, and I didn't have the heart to stab him in the back with the new information Saint and I have—nor do either of us have a death wish.

Revealing Luca is gay would be one—for us and potentially him too. It would also be pretty fucking low and inhuman. I wouldn't stoop to that. Ever.

Things are safe right now. Easy. There's no reason to stir the pot.

Dani shakes her head. "I still can't believe you turned in the article then quit."

I laugh and lean back in my chair as I look around at my new office at the Hawkeye Club. "Oh, come on. You hated working for Doug, too. And even though he loved the article, he had no intention of ever giving me a promotion. He has me pigeonholed pretty solidly as a nonsense fluff reporter, and I'm not going to give him the satisfaction of watching me suffer in that role for the rest of my career. Working on press releases and ad copy for Savage and Gabe is a much better option."

No one was happy when they learned what I had done, but once I got them to sit down and listen to what I had to say about Luca, tensions eased—sort of.

Savage and Gabe, and Saint for that matter, still have concerns about my safety—no matter how many times I tell them I trust Luca—so Savage offered me the job, mostly so I'd be in the same building and would be easier to keep an eye on—though no one will ever admit that.

I turned it down, of course.

Some part of me hoped Doug would see the light and give me the promotion, but when it became clear he wouldn't, I told him to publish the article and that I was done. I've never seen a human face turn that red before, and the vitriol he spewed at me on my way out the door rivals anything I've ever heard. But...it was the best decision I've ever made.

This place with these people is home.

Dani grins at me. "Plus, it makes it a lot easier for you and Saint to have a little afternoon delight in his office right down the hall."

I laugh and nod as my body heats at the memory of him bending me over his desk yesterday. "Well, there's that too."

Everyone knew what we were doing, but the fact that Savage and Dani and Gabe and Skye all have a habit of doing the exact same thing means that sex in the workplace isn't really a problem when you're employed by the Hawkes.

"I just wish I would have thought of this before." Dani rises to her feet. "It just never occurred to me that having somebody on full-time and in-house who can handle any writing stuff would be a good idea."

I shrug and rise to my feet. "Better late than never."

She throws her hair back over her shoulder. "I have to go. Kennedy is at Mom's, but I need to pick her up."

"All right, I'll talk to you later."

With a quick blown kiss over her shoulder, she dashes out the door, and I drop back down into my chair.

You made the right choice, Care.

The article is good. I'm not just patting myself on the back, either. Luca has been willing to reveal all kinds of information I never thought he would to create a truly enlightening social interest piece. And everyone in New Orleans is eating up the chance to learn more about its newest mafia king. The hundreds of unopened emails and voicemails asking to talk to me only confirm what I already know. I nailed it.

But leaving the paper was right for me. This is where I belong. With the Hawkes and Saint.

"Caroline?"

I turn to the door. Byron stands just inside the jamb, his hair in disarray and dark bags under his eyes.

Jesus.

"Byron, are you okay?"

He shuts the door behind him, unfolds a copy of the *Times,* and drops it on my desk. I look down at the page.

My article?

"Care, we need to talk."

SAINT

"Well, it's my understanding her ex violated his parole and is getting sent back to prison, so there shouldn't really be any issue anymore."

Vance sighs into the phone. "I agree, but she still asked to come work at TWO instead of staying at the main club."

Fuck.

I run my hand back over my head. This call from Vance was the last thing I needed today. This is the kind of stuff Byron usually handles, but he's been MIA for two days. It's very unusual for him, and that has set my skin crawling and left a nagging feeling in the back of my head that something is up.

Something not good.

The only thing that's kept Savage and Gabe from sending out a damn search party for him is that he's only technically missed *one* shift. Though, if he doesn't show today, I wouldn't be surprised if the National Guard was sent out after him.

This is his domain—dealing with the dancers and their schedules. I deal with their security. Which doesn't appear to be the issue even though Scarlett's ex has caused issues in the past, before I started working here.

We need Byron. He's the best at talking to and dealing with

the girls. They trust him and open up to him about whatever is going on with them. And this isn't just a little personnel issue either. This is *Scarlett*.

She's been at the club for years, and she's a favorite for some of our regulars. If she takes off to work at TWO, we may lose a lot of really good customers at this location. TWO is on the other side of town, and most of our regulars live over here. She's a big draw, and we don't want to lose her. Her sudden desire to leave is unsettling to say the least.

"I'll talk to her. If she still wants to go over there after we talk, then I won't fight her on it. We don't want to lose her completely. But Savage and Gabe will want to talk to her too, if it comes to that."

"Sounds good, Saint. Thank you. I miss having you over here every day."

I chuckle and lean back in my chair. "Yeah, me too. Sort of. But I have to say, working at a desk is a lot better than working at the door."

My job at TWO was easy. Stand by the door. Look intimidating. Throw out anyone who crosses the line.

Easy, but not the most thrilling job in the world, or one that utilized my other talents.

He laughs. "No doubt. Talk to you later, big guy."

Hopefully not about this. Byron will come back and deal with it so I can concentrate on my job—keeping the clubs and everyone in them secure.

While things may have quieted down with Luca since Caroline's article, that doesn't mean there aren't hundreds of other things to be vigilant about. And I won't make a mistake again like the one that almost cost Storm her life.

My phone barely hits the cradle before Caroline appears at the door with her lip pulled between her teeth.

That's never good.

"What is it, babe?"

She glances behind her into the hallway. "Byron has something he needs to talk to all of us about. I think it's best to do it in Savage's office."

Well, shit.

My bad feeling was right. First, he disappears for an entire day, and now, he's returned and brought something he needs to tell all of us. It has to be something serious. The guy is the most reliable employee I've ever seen. He's hardworking and doesn't create problems where there aren't any. This does not bode well.

"Okay, I'm coming."

I shove away from my desk and make my way to the door. Caroline waits for me, and I lean down and press a kiss on top of her head.

"You okay?"

She nods and glances at Byron.

Jesus. He looks like shit.

He won't even make eye-contact with me as we make our way down to Savage's office.

Fuck. This is really bad.

The door is open, and Gabe leans over Savage's desk examining something laid out across it.

"Guys, you got a minute?"

They both look up with their eyes narrowed on us.

Savage waves us in. "Sure, what's up?"

Byron steps in behind me.

All eyes move to him.

Everyone's been worried, and Gabe has been ready to send out a goddamn search party since this morning. Looks like we had reason to be concerned though.

My gut twists as we all walk in and settle into the chairs.

Byron moves to stand at the side of Savage's desk where we can all see him. He keeps his head dropped to the floor as he holds up a copy of the *Times* that's open to Caroline's article.

He swallows and looks around the room, finally meeting

everyone's eyes with his red, bloodshot ones. "We need to talk about Luca, or as I first knew him, Steele."

I hope you enjoyed *Tainted Saint*! Click here to get an exclusive BONUS SCENE with Saint and Caroline on St. Patrick's Day! https://BookHip.com/TPNADAB

ABOUT THE AUTHOR

Gwyn McNamee is an attorney, writer, wife, and mother (to one human baby and two fur babies). Originally from the Midwest, Gwyn relocated to her husband's home town of Las Vegas in 2015 and is enjoying her respite from the cold and snow. Gwyn has been writing down her crazy stories and ideas for years and finally decided to share them with the world. She loves to write stories with a bit of suspense and action mingled with romance and heat.

When she isn't either writing or voraciously devouring any books she can get her hands on, Gwyn is busy adding to her tattoo collection, golfing, and stirring up trouble with her perfect mix of sweetness and sarcasm (usually while wearing heels).

Gwyn loves to hear from her readers. Here is where you can find her:

FB Reader Group: https://www.facebook.com/groups/1667380963540655/

Newsletter: www.gwynmcnamee.com/newsletter

Website: http://www.gwynmcnamee.com/

Facebook: https://www.facebook.com/AuthorGwynMcNamee/

Twitter: https://twitter.com/GwynMcNamee

Instagram: https://www.instagram.com/gwynmcnamee

Bookbub: https://www.bookbub.com/authors/gwynmcnamee

OTHER WORKS BY GWYN MCNAMEE

Billionaires of New Orleans:

The Hawke Family Series

Savage Collision (The Hawke Family - Book One)

He's everything she didn't know she wanted. She's everything he thought he could never have.

The last thing I expect when I walk into The Hawkeye Club is to fall head over heels in lust. It's supposed to be a rescue mission. I have to get my baby sister off the pole, into some clothes, and out of the grasp of the pussy peddler who somehow manipulated her into stripping. But the moment I see Savage Hawke and verbally spar with him, my ability to remain rational flies out the window and my libido takes center stage. I've never wanted a relationship—my time is better spent focusing on taking down the scum running this city—but what I want and what I need are apparently two different things.

Danika Eriksson storms into my office in her high heels and on her high horse. Her holier-than-thou attitude and accusations should offend me, but instead, I can't get her out of my head or my heart. Her incomparable drive, take-no prisoners attitude, and blatant honesty captivate me and hold me prisoner. I should steer clear, but my self-preservation instinct is apparently dead—which is exactly what our relationship will be once she knows everything. It's only a matter of time.

The truth doesn't always set you free. Sometimes, it just royally screws you.

AVAILABLE AT ALL RETAILERS:

Tortured Skye (The Hawke Family - Book Two)

She's always been off-limits. He's always just out of reach.

Falling in love with Gabe Anderson was as easy as breathing. Fighting my feelings for my brother's best friend was agonizingly hard. I never imagined giving in to my desire for him would cause such a destructive ripple effect. That kiss was my grasp at a lifeline—something, anything to hold me steady in my crumbling life. Now, I have to suffer with the fallout while trying to convince him it's all worth the consequences.

Guilt overwhelms me—over what I've done, the lives I've taken, and more than anything, over my feelings for Skye Hawke. Craving my best friend's little sister is insanely self-destructive. It never should have happened, but since the moment she kissed me, I haven't been able to get her out of my mind. If I take what I want, I risk losing everything. If I don't, I'll lose her and a piece of myself. The raging storm threatening to rain down on the city is nothing compared to the one that will come from my decision.

Love can be torture, but sometimes, love is the only thing that can save you.

AVAILABLE AT ALL RETAILERS:

Books2read.com/Tortured-Skye

Stone Sober (The Hawke Family - Book Three)

She's innocent and sweet. He's dark and depraved.

Stone Hawke is precisely the kind of man women are warned about— handsome, intelligent, arrogant, and intricately entangled with some dangerous people. I should stay away, but he manages to strip my soul bare with just a look and dominates my thoughts. Bad decisions are in my past. My life is (mostly) on track, even if it is no longer the one to medical school. I can't allow myself to cave to the fierce pull and ardent attraction I feel toward the youngest Hawke.

Nora Eriksson is off-limits, and not just because she's my brother's employee and sister-in-law. Despite the fact she's stripping at The Hawkeye Club, she has an innocent and pure heart. Normally, the only thing that appeals to me about innocence is the opportunity to taint it. But not when it comes to Nora. I can't expose her to the filth permeating my life. There are too many things I can't control, things completely out of my hands. She doesn't deserve any of it, but the power she holds over me is stronger than any addiction.

The hardest battles we fight are often with ourselves, but only through defeating our own demons can we find true peace.

AVAILABLE AT ALL RETAILERS:

books2read.com/StoneSober

Building Storm (The Hawke Family - Book Four)

She hasn't been living. He's looking for a way to forget it all.

My life went up in flames. All I'm left with is my daughter and ashes. The simple act of breathing is so excruciating, there are days I wish I could stop altogether. So I have no business being at the party, and I definitely shouldn't be in the arms of the handsome stranger. When his lips meet mine, he breathes life into me for the first time since the day the inferno disintegrated my world. But loving again isn't in the cards, and there are even greater dangers to face than trying to keep Landon McCabe out of my heart.

Running is my only option. I have to get away from Chicago and the betrayal that shattered my world. I need a new life-one without attachments. The vibrancy of New Orleans convinces me it's possible to start over. Yet in all the excitement of a new city, it's Storm Hawke's dark, sad beauty that draws me in. She isn't looking for love, and we both need a hot, sweaty release without feelings getting involved. But even the best laid plans fail, and life can leave you burned.

Love can build, and love can destroy. But in the end, love is what raises you from the ashes.

AVAILABLE AT ALL RETAILERS:

books2read.com/BuildingStorm

Tainted Saint (The Hawke Family - Book Five)

He's searching for absolution. She wants her happily ever after.

Solomon Clarke goes by Saint, though he's anything but. After lusting for him from afar, the masquerade party affords me the anonymity to pursue that attraction without worrying about the fall-out of hooking-up with the bouncer from the Hawkeye Club. From the second he lays his eyes and hands on me, I'm helpless to resist him. Even burying myself in a dangerous investigation can't erase the memory of our combustible connection and one night together. The only problem... he has no idea who I am.

Caroline Brooks thinks I don't see her watching me, the way her eyes rake over me with appreciation. But I've noticed, and the party is the perfect opportunity to unleash the desire I've kept reined in for so damn long. It also sets off a series of events no one sees coming. Events that leave those I love hurting because of my failures. While the guilt eats away at my soul, Caroline continues to weigh on my heart. That woman may be the death of me, but oh, what a way to go.

Life isn't always clean, and sometimes, it takes a saint to do the dirty work.

AVAILABLE AT ALL RETAILERS:

books2read.com/TaintedSaint

Steele Resolve (The Hawke Family - Book Six)

For one man, power is king. For the other, loyalty reigns.

Mob boss Luca "Steele" Abello isn't just dangerous—he's lethal. A master manipulator, liar, and user, no one should trust a word that comes out of his mouth. Yet, I can't get him out of my head. The time we spent together before I knew his true identity is seared into my brain. His touch. His voice. They haunt my every waking hour and occupy my dreams. So does my guilt. I'm literally sleeping with the enemy and betraying the only family I've ever had. When I come clean, it will be the end of me.

Byron Harris is a distraction I can't afford. I never should have let it go beyond that first night, but I couldn't stay away. Even when I learned who he was, when the *only* option was to end things, I kept going back, risking his life and mine to continue our indiscretion. The truth of what I am could get us both killed, but being with the man who's such an integral part of the Hawke family is even more terrifying. The only people I've ever cared about are on opposing sides, and I'm the rift that could end their friendship forever.

Love is a battlefield isn't just a saying. For some, it's a reality.

AVAILABLE AT ALL RETAILERS:

books2read.com/SteeleResolve

Then check out the Billionaires of New Orleans: The Hawke Family Second Generation Series to meet the children of the original characters!